Sunshine & Sabotage

A Small Town, Boy Next Door Romance

Annie Rae

Rae of Romance, LLC

Contents

Prologue

Melanie

"**A**re you fucking kidding me?"

A feminine screech follows the crack in my voice, but I can't care about the naked bimbo scrambling for the sheet to cover her chest... our sheet.

"What are you doing here?" Aaron scrambles off the screaming woman like she's radioactive, his face full of more accusation than guilt.

My mouth drops, fury thumping deafening blood through my ears. I never, even in my worst nightmares, expected to find my fiancé in bed with another woman... hours after our engagement party.

"I brought you cake, since you had to leave the party. It's in the kitchen... FYI." Venom drips from every syllable.

"You left my mother to clean up the party," he says, his voice full of disdain.

"You seriously blaming me for this?" I wave at the strewn bedroom, crinkling my nose at the disgusting stench of sex in the air.

I don't expect an answer. Of course, he blames me. Aaron is nothing if not a coward.

"Who the hell is she?" skinny Barbie howls, near tears.

Okay. At least blondie didn't knowingly break up a marriage. Although, we're not married yet.

Thank God!

Somehow, Aaron has the nerve to stand beside the bed, acting as sheepish as a little boy caught stealing cookies.

Out of pity, I address the girl, shoving down the shame threatening to swallow me whole. "I am his *ex*-fiancée... the woman who put up with his mother's demands for our wedding over the last three months. The one he left at dinner tonight because his little brother—who was supposed to be at our party—needed a drunk ride."

Pissed, I turn to Aaron, my fist clenching at my sides. His hands drop to guard his balls. Like there's anything there worth saving. "Did Matt even need a ride?"

His face reddens. That man hates losing the upper hand, and obviously, I just bust his lie wide open.

"I should have never given you a key." Angrily, he jerks his clothes from the floor, struggling to shove his leg through those stupid happy face boxers.

If chopping his penis off didn't sound wonderful right now, I'd laugh at the clumsy picture. Poor little wilting erection...

Aaron catches me looking at his penis with pity and growls. "What the fuck you looking at?"

The frazzled girl rushes off the bed, wrapping her body in our sheet—Aaron's sheet, not mine. She won't meet my eye. "I'm sorry. I didn't know."

Her apology eases some of the lava flowing through my veins. Just a touch. Although, nodding is all I can manage as I watch her scurry to the attached bathroom with her discarded clothes.

Before she slams the door, she takes one last scan of Aaron and mumbles, "so not worth it."

Hysterical laughter bubbles up and I shake my head at the irony. "Right there with ya, sister."

With a critical eye, I look around the bedroom I never quite moved into. One of my books sits on the nightstand. A pair of shoes and a few outfits are all I have in the closet. My eyes fall on Aaron. I never quite had him, either.

I shake my head. "After everything I did for you."

He scoffs. "You're lucky I proposed, chubs. If Grandmother hadn't pushed me to settle down..."

Ouch.

Unfortunately, I can't hide my flinch fast enough, and Aaron smirks. He hit his mark.

Thankfully, months of schooling my expression with his mom have taught me. I bite the back of my tongue, drawing on the disgust boiling deep in my gut to focus on the flaws slapping me in the face and not the man I loved.

Aaron thinks he's God's gift to women. *Newsflash, buddy... you're not.*

Instead of a handsome, well-put-together man, I see the facade.

Aaron's a dick. Constantly ridiculing my weight, never admitting the dad bod he slipped into—minus the kids. He's spoiled. A lazy, pompous ass! He leaves his towels and underwear on the floor, probably because he knows I hate it. Every weekend, his mom cooks him dinners for the week, sometimes even grocery shopping, delivering, and unpacking the shit for him, too.

He's almost thirty and can't fucking adult.

Deciding I've given this man enough of my time, I tilt my head high and grab my book on the nightstand. He will not win. I'll send for my clothes, but why waste a good romance? Just because my prince turned out to be a toad...

Hell, the book-gasms on those steamy pages were the only ones happening in that bed.

A doorhandle jiggles, the sound jarring in the silent bedroom. Aside from Aaron scrambling to get dressed now that his sidepiece locked him out of the bathroom, the room is still. A tomb. I'd laugh if my heart and my future hadn't just crumbled like a Fabergé egg.

On the way out, a strike of Grinch slaps away my restraint and I rotate on a heel, facing down the man I turned my life upside down for. I feel... nothing.

Well, not nothing.

Narrowing my eyes at the shelf by my head, I upend the stash of Aaron's pride and joy, equestrian trophies. He spent two hours hanging that thing when he moved in. He wouldn't even give me a wall for my diploma, because as he said... *I don't live here yet.* And that makes the smack of my hand against the polished mahogany as satisfying as a New Year's Kiss... another thing I won't be getting this year either.

On my way out the door, with the tiny Christmas tree I decorated mocking me from the corner, I slam the congratulatory cake I brought Aaron against the wall. The streak of icing across the paint is little consolation as I close the door on my dreams for a family anytime soon.

Chapter One

Melanie

Weeks later, with a legal ultimatum burning a hole in my pocket, I yank the front door open of Fresh Kiss Coffee. *"Goddamn his nerve."* The heavenly scent of fancy coffee doesn't even dent my sour mood.

"Problem, hun?" Gary, the flamboyant shop owner, grins over the glass display. I step closer, eyeing the tray of breakfast sandwiches he passes to the barista behind him. "Box those up for Tuck." He beams when the young girl hustles like an eager beaver with young twenty-something's energy.

"Those look yum."

Gary's chest puffs with pride. "They are, but I can't sell an egg croissant after lunch for the life of me." He folds wiry arms over the high counter and offers a friendly customer service smile. The same one I display for potential clients.

"Seems like a waste of such pretty food." Not to mention, the late morning offerings in the display are slim.

"It would be, except the local restaurants send our leftovers to the VFW building for their evening classes and meetings."

"Wow! That's really nice." This town's generosity is beyond. It's a big reason I stayed. However, I can't process failing on one more front in the picture-perfect little town. Being the odd man out in a place where everyone knows everybody. Where bright smiles shine while mine rings false. People here love their happy homes and jobs, while I flail, homeless and rudderless.

'The letter' blares every mistake I made in my relationship, including the worst one of agreeing to marry Aaron in the first place. The quaint coffee shop offers a brief escape before I deal with that fall out. No outside stresses.

"Why the frown, little lady?" At my elbow, a familiar older lady grins up at me from under cat-eye glasses. *How do I know her?*

Oh, shit! She was at the stripper party the ladies threw as a wedding shower. For a failed wedding.

My face heats.

"Hi, Ms. Betsy." Her eyes soften as she bumps into my shoulder, barely higher than her own.

Great! I'm no taller than an eighty-year-old shrunken woman.

Gary looks up as Betsy sidles up to my side with a wide smile. "What can I get for you two beautiful ladies this morning?"

Betsy chuckles, waggling her eyebrows my way. "This one's a charmer. You watch out for him, deary."

Gary chuckles and wraps up something from the glass case I don't see—and Betsy never ordered. He passes her goodies over the counter with a cinnamon scented tea—prepared by his quick-eyed employee—and a grin splitting his angular cheeks. "Here you go, you minx. Don't go spilling my secrets to new people in town."

"Oh, she's not new, honey. Our Melanie is here to stay." Betsy winks at me before digging a few bills from her giant, Golden Girl style purse and collecting her goodies. Her eyes harden on me. "As for you, Missy, you let us know what you need. References. Girls' night out. Help burying a body. This town's got your back."

My brows hit my hairline and Gary chuckles. The bells tinkle, signaling Betsy's exit before my brain catches up to what she said. Only then do I turn back, my mouth snapping closed as the sympathetic barista smiles gently.

"Can I have two eclairs and a coffee? Cream and sugar. To-go, please."

As I wait, my gaze catches the cork board advertising lost kitties, babysitters, and random flyers. I finger a phone number, selling a shiny baby grand that resembles the antique upright I learned on as a young girl. If I ever manage to right my life and have a home of my own, I want a piece like this with history. Not shiny and new.

Sighing, I move down the board, searching for any notice for a roommate. An apartment vacancy. Anything. I've been at the bed-and-breakfast since finding Aaron in bed. Returning to his mother's house for my stuff, facing that ridicule, seems impossible until I have somewhere to go.

The paper in front of my face warbles as my eyes glaze. Whatever crumb of energy I had drained at Betsy's reminder of how different this week would have been.

My wedding week.

Instead of pity, Betsy would have grilled me for details of my honeymoon. Her sad eyes would have shined with the naughty innuendos the little old lady is famous for. She'd have commented on my tan in the middle of a Kentucky frost-bitten January.

"Umm... Melanie?" A tap on my shoulder startles me nearly out of my skin. My name is pure velvet, purred from the sexiest man I've ever laid eyes on.

How does the hot guy know my name?

Over-friendly Gary grins over the counter and I realize he's been calling my name.

"Sorry." I rush to grab my bag of goodies and lean down, hiding the ruddiness in my cheeks with a sip of mind-saving caffeine.

"Distracted?" Handsome asks before ordering a very basic, utilitarian coffee and Gary gives us his back to fiddle with a fancy silver machine.

"Five minutes, Tyler."

"No rush." Tyler tosses a polite wave, his focus annoyingly steady... on me. "Looks like I've got a bit of time."

Embarrassed, I step away, assuming he's making polite conversation. "Enjoy." The last impression I want to give my new town—especially Aaron's hometown—is that I'm flighty... or an airhead.

But I'm a bit confused. Why is a guy who looks like this talking to the chubby girl?

Are small towns really *this* nice?

Tucking the travel containers under my arm, I snatch the lone flyer offering a rental on the outskirts of town and scan the details. My parting smile feels fake as hell, but I need to hurry if I'm going to check out this place before I meet Liza for lunch. Her friendship motivated me to stay in town. Well, her and that I gave up everything in the city when I moved closer for Aaron.

The address in my hand is farther away than I'd like, but I must check every option. My pay-by-the-night stay at the bed-and-breakfast is over at the end of the week, so I'm in a crunch. The owners have a large wedding party coming in and need my room by next week. Plus, not a single part of me wants to talk to happy wedding guests over the breakfast table.

"Looking for a place?"

Startled, I jerk, realizing Tyler walks in step beside me. "Uh, yeah." I wave the paper in my hand like the biggest dork and cringe. Heat rushes up my neck. *Real smooth, Mel.*

He chuckles. "Have a minute?"

"I should get going…" My eyes fall on the advertisement in my hand and back to Gary prepping his coffee.

"Oh, come on. You wouldn't leave me lonely in the new year."

I stare, realizing the shop is mostly empty at this time of day. I don't know what to say.

"Come on. I don't bite… much." He winks and pulls out a chair at a close bistro. A hand waves at the spot across from him, his face open, hopeful.

Curiosity gets the better of me. Or maybe that impossible smile. What hot blooded woman could resist that temptation? Not one who hasn't had a non-self-induced orgasm since Justin Bieber had a baby face. Since Kanye and Kim debated on which direction to name their kid.

So, I sit.

Despite having no time for men after jumping off Aaron's roller coaster. Or the far-fetched idea that a dude with that body and those dimples would show interest. I'm down on myself, but come on...

Curiosity gets the best of me. "How did you know my name?"

To my surprise, those angular cheeks tint, giving him an adorable quality that shakes a bit of the nerves clogging my brain.

Liza will understand if I'm a few minutes late. Especially for a tall, dark, and handsome delay.

"I'm friends with Smith." His awkward pause confirms he knows the state of my f-ed up life.

Great.

Something about that sits wrong. I don't want the town pitying me. Nor every attractive man to see the woman who got played, who fell for a smooth talker's slick lies.

Won't happen again.

That's all I can think of. With Adele's dulcet tones piping through the speakers, amping up the romance, denying the pull of those soft brown eyes seems impossible. So, I'll sit with as much smoothness as a drunk penguin walking a tightrope.

The urge to tuck tail and run is huge. Disappear back to the city. Hide in plain sight, where no one knows—or cares—about my failed love life. Hiding in one of those remote cabins at the hot springs may be a better plan, but I gave myself six months. If I can't make a new life here work... my business, friends, a home... everything, then I'll admit defeat and head back to the city. After everything, I can't let go of the fantasy I built in my head. That quiet, simple life. No smog. No crowds. No crazy.

"Smith is an amazing chef," I say, fighting my tongue-tiedness.

A smile tilts the corner of Tyler's lips. "He is. I've been addicted to the man's food since he rocked the hell out of that hot plate in barracks."

My eyes widen. "Is that allowed?"

He shrugs. "I never saw a thing..."

Tyler pauses while Gary drops his coffee and treats at our table, dropping a sneaky thumbs up at the side of his hip that Tyler can't see. My mouth falls. I want to glare, ask what the hell that look is about, but Gary's gone before I can. When he's gone, Tyler's rich baritone drops conspiratorially low, and he leans all the way over the table, closing the space. "Neither did anyone else, as long as

Smith kept our battalion fed. That man can butter up anyone with his S'mores popcorn."

I chuckle, nearly choking on a mouthful of coffee. "I doubt you complained…"

"Hell no! A growing boy's gotta eat." Humor lights his eyes as he pats a maddeningly flat stomach. That T-shirt does nothing to hide the firmness underneath. There's not an inch of fluff to be found. Damn him.

I look down at my thighs, and then at the wrapped treats I will not be eating in front of this specimen. A very unladylike snort slips out. "No way you eat Smith's food. Everything I tasted at Christmas would add ten pounds if left unsupervised for half an hour."

Tyler's grin widens, catching the hidden compliment.

Back track! "I uh… you just…" I can't tell the man he's too freaking hot to eat any of the full-flavored perfection Smith cooked for my failed wedding shower. "Uh, never mind." I shake my head and move to stand up, but a hand holds me in place.

Expressive brown eyes scan my face. It's a little unnerving, except the friendliness mirrored back feels like a long-lost friend. "I'm sorry. I was just trying to make you laugh." His shoulders hold tight as I work through my options. A smart woman would be out of here—self-preservation at its finest—yet, for some reason, my feet don't move. "How have you been... after?"

There it is... the question I've hidden from for weeks.

Liza, Smith, and a few times Lennox, are the only people I've seen since my life fell off a cliff. Although, anti-social doesn't work if I'm setting up a business here.

I sit up straighter, dragging strength in a heavy breath. *Fake it 'til you make it,* mama always said.

"It's a new year." I shrug, as if that's all that matters. "How did the holidays treat you?"

Tyler looks torn. He sees through the mask, but surprisingly, that doesn't irk me as much as I'd expect. Kindness radiates from his eyes. So different that Aaron's narcissistic stare. That man always picked at anything he saw as weakness. Calculated criticisms were his bread and butter.

I barely know him, but Tyler's easy-going nature is why I haven't run out of this quaint coffee shop. Even though sitting with a stranger, especially a cute one, triggers my self-consciousness.

"Holidays were good. Work. The festival. Same ole, same ole." A slight ruddiness colors his cheeks, piquing my curiosity.

I cock my head, unsure of what to say.

Our table falls into an awkward silence.

"Anything else I can get you guys?" Gary eagerly awaits at the edge of our table, eyeing us like the latest celebrity gossip on Page Six. His grin beams, catching Tyler's attention, who pauses, cup halfway to his lips.

He glances my way and I shake my head.

"We're good," he says to the shop owner.

Gary nods but makes no move to go about his business.

Tyler lifts a brow. "Anything else, G?"

"No. No..." Gary backs away, cheesing ear to ear. "You all... enjoy."

Tyler eyes me nervously. "So, uh, small towns, huh?"

I smirk. "Is it always like this?"

Our heads turn, finding Gary leaned against the counter on folded arms. His overeager attention is locked on us instead of anything restaurant related at all.

"I'm going to say no. Otherwise, I have a feeling you'll run right out that door and never look back."

Warmth floods through my chest that Tyler would care if I stay or go. It's preposterous. "Yeah, good idea." Gary catches my eye, waggling his eyebrows excitedly. *Holy shit!*

Shyness takes over, my gaze dropping to the extremely fascinating cup of coffee in my hand. Yes. Vanilla goodness. That's where I should focus. Not the hard body with the soft brown eyes shining like his life smells of rainbow farts and unicorn kisses.

The flyer on the table brings my focus back to the fact that my life is very much *not* rainbow farts and unicorn kisses.

"I probably should get going," I say, fully aware that sitting for five minutes screams fickle. Instead, I focus on gathering my small belongings to stand. "I've got appointments today. Errands to run. You know." Really… what's the point of staying? Chatting up a hot guy is not on my to-do list. Getting my life in order is.

Tyler's smile fades as he leans back in the too-small-for-his-bulk wooden chair. A creak startles him forward and I almost grin until his head nods at the paper in my hand. "You looking for a place?"

The advertisement details a two-bedroom space on the outskirts of town. It literally says space… not apartment or house. And there are no photos, just a seven-digit number to call for an appointment and bullet point text touting a full shower as its selling factor.

Are there such things as a partial shower? Half shower? Shower shell? What are we talking about here?

"Yeah, I'm staying at the Inn until I find a more permanent lease."

Folding the paper, I hide my bare-bottom option. Pure desperation and a piddly sum in my bank account have led to this situation. Too many wasted wedding expenses, like the wedding dress packed in a storage unit one town over, keeping my furniture company. For all I care, the mice can eat it. Renting a space seemed safer while I bunked with Aaron's parents, because no way was I dumping an apartment's worth of furniture the way Aaron wanted. It took years of saving to accumulate my favorite pieces. They may not be fancy, or up to his standards, but they were mine.

"So, you're staying in town?" Tyler asks, ripping me from the rabbit hole I'd fallen down.

"That's the plan." He returns my smile, the corners of his eyes crinkling adorably. *I need to go.* Tyler is… too much "Thanks for, uh… hanging out."

Gathering my resolve—and my food—I leave before I get too comfortable. I've got a big mess to straighten out and little time to do it.

Chapter Two

Melanie

The door is a football field away for someone attempting a graceful, non-stumbling idiot exit in front of a man capable of igniting a dormant volcano.

Unfortunately, my shoes squeak in my hurry for the door, making a classy exit impossible. Tyler's chair legs screech as he stands up as well. *Shit.*

"Don't follow. Don't follow," I whisper, my heart fluttering as I reach for the handle, only to have it ripped out of my hand. *"Ahh!"* The shift jerks me off balance and I stumble, nearly toppling an older, blonde-headed woman.

"Well!" she huffs, obviously put-out by my accidental appearance. Oversized, tortoise-shell glasses magnify her startled eyes. "Watch where you're going, young lady."

My mouth gapes before I can regain my composure. Snapping my lips closed, I straighten my back to give this snarky old woman a piece of my mind, but before I can, a hand lands on my lower back and ushers me through the door.

"Morning, Ms. Peggy." Tyler's rich southern drawl soothes as he quickly shoos me across the sidewalk. "Hurry."

"Watch it!" I slap at his heavy palm. I'm going to give another person a lesson in politeness if he doesn't stop pushing me.

"Tyler, you be careful with these new... people moving into our town. Your daddy would hate to see you twisted all up over some harlot."

"A wha—" I flip around. Forget the forty-year age difference. "How dare—" Tyler cuts me off, stepping in my path to block the view of Ms. Blue Hair Bug-Eyes. His thick forearm locks across my middle, holding me in place.

Tyler's head drops close to my ear. "She's just the town kook, Melanie. Ignore her." He plasters on a fake smile for the old woman. "We're good, Ms. P. I'll tell my dad you said hi." His wave is as friendly as ever as he grabs my elbow and steers me away from the old bat who huffs like a bull storming Pamplona.

"I feel sorry for Gary," I say as she disappears into the once-peaceful coffee shop.

Tyler chuckles, maneuvering us around clumps of melted snow on the sidewalk. By the time I snap out of my tantrum, we're standing in front of a black truck. A vintage Grandpa-era truck that gleams brand new.

"You okay?"

I swallow. "Yes. I just…" I wave the advertisement in my hand and sigh. "I should get going,"

"That place is a shit hole," he says, crossing those muscular arms over his Henley.

"This?"

"Yes!" The annoyance in his voice surprises me and I wince. "Sorry. Just… the place hasn't been painted since before I was born. The roof leaks. The windows would fall out with a stiff breeze. And that's just the outside. Old man Leary doesn't have the cash to fix it up. I've patched things here and there, but he sold his farm after his first heart attack. Now he's trying to pass that old pack house off as a rental to supplement his disability check. It's sad."

"Aww, damn." My shoulders sag. "If I go see this little old man, I'm going to be guilted into renting, aren't I?"

Tyler nods, his smile brightening. "Come with me, instead."

"Why?" The question is harsher than intended, but Tyler isn't offended. In fact, he laughs.

"I've got a way better idea."

"For an apartment?"

"Yes. It's close. One bedroom, but the living room is a good size if you need space for an office."

"Where?" I wrack my brain. "I've checked every listing there is online, and a few *winners* in person. There's nothing in my price range left."

"This one isn't listed yet." He smiles expectantly, but I don't get it. "Look, you and Liza are friends, right?" I nod. "It's Smith's place."

I stare dumbfounded. I haven't spread the word about the state of my messed-up life after the breakup. Part of me wanted to get settled in town and pretend like I'm not flying by the seat of my pants.

Tyler grabs the flyer from my hand. "Smith hasn't given up his lease yet, but he's practically living at the farm already." His voice softens. "More room for him and the baby."

"I met her," I say, my throat clogging up.

That sweet, abandoned little girl distracted everyone in town when she showed up. A blessing, considering it was the same time Aaron's mother started spreading lies about our breakup. Liza brought the baby to breakfast with me at the diner, us both bonding over idiots not worthy of our stress.

She's been such a gift to that little girl after the biological mother dropped the teeny tiny life in their lap. Both new parents have stepped up, despite their shock, so Fiona will never have to deal with her mother's dysfunctional lifestyle. One breakfast with those adorable cheeks sent my ovaries into acrobatics. Not that my plans for the quaint 2.5 kids, a Labradoodle... the whole shebang, are anywhere on my radar now.

I glance across the street to the sprawling park where the Christmas Festival gave me a peek at the wholesome family fun this town offers. A tease, of course. Not for me. But I still want to give the town a chance.

"You okay?"

My gaze jerks to Tyler's, concern creasing his brow I don't want to deal with.

"I'm good. Great." My voice cracks, but I swallow that useless pain, plastering on the smile that's worked for weeks. "Can we tour this super-secret lease? Or should I schedule with Smith...?"

"No. No," he rushes. "I got you. Like I said, it's not far." Reaching around me, he opens the passenger door to his shiny truck and waits. "Hop up. I'll drop you at your car after."

Bossy, much?

Yes, it's hot, but the part of me tired of high-handed men wants to call Tyler out for the assumption. Unfortunately, his sexiness wins, and I end up using the offered hand to climb into the cab. The scent of pine, leather… all things outdoorsy man, torment me as I watch those spectacular muscles jog around the front of the truck and join me on today's one-eighty shift of plans.

Chapter Three

Tyler

When I lift a hand to knock, I swallow a truckload of nerves over the little spitfire standing by my side.

The woman turns me into a godforsaken schoolboy. I'm a grown man. I've got a job... two, actually. I've seen war. Lost friends. My little house is a little fixer upper. But what else would the town's handyman own?

She fidgets at my side, until the sound of boots stops just inside the door, a raucous laugh hitting us the moment the door rips open.

My best friend looks nothing like himself. "What the hell is that?" I ask, pointing at the giant grin spreading across his face.

Smith stops. "What?" He glances behind him, his back stiffening, I assume, imagining his daughter is into something non-baby proofed.

"That smile, man." I slap my buddy on the shoulder, walking past him for the little princess babbling in her exerciser. She bounces in the round contraption, surrounded by toys and noise makers that thrill the little girl to no end. That gummy smile wraps me further around the little finger, now slobber-covered and wiggling excitedly in my direction.

I always wanted one of these.

Since my best friend's daughter showed up in his lap, it's been at the forefront of my brain. All the things missing in my life.

"A. Ba. Ba. Ba," she chatters, twisting my heart in the best ways. The sweet girl doesn't care that she's surrounded by moving boxes. She's pure happiness.

"Dude! She's grown so much in two weeks. What the hell are you feeding this chick?" Smith chuckles as Fiona grabs my outstretched finger and brings it to her mouth.

"What can I say? I'm a chef. I like feeding my women."

Liza aims a sharp eye at Smith. "Don't you know you don't comment on a woman's weight?"

He wraps her waist with one of those NC-17 looks that have become commonplace since their relationship went from non-existent to hyper speed.

"Stop it," she hiss-whispers, stifling a giggle when Smith grabs her ass, his self-satisfied grin not looking the least bit ashamed.

I glance at Melanie standing just inside the door and fight a smile. Her face flushes just as a sharp pinch on my thumb jerks my head to the tiny shrapnel gnawing my flesh. "You little pipsqueak. Why d'ya bite your uncle Ty?"

"Maybe she heard you call her fat?" Liza wrestles away from Smith with a smirk and walks around me to wrap Melanie's neck in a hug. "Come on in," she says, dragging her into the room.

"I did not call her fat." Standing from my crouched place, I shake out my finger, eyeing the darling in question. "I didn't call you anything, did I, my sweet little chunky muffin? Men love curves on a woman."

"Hah!" A loud guffaw smothers before it's all the way out, bringing all eyes to Melanie. She turns an even darker shade of crimson, so I let the laugh slide, not wanting a confrontation in front of our friends. And because of her recent stresses. Still, I won't have Melanie questioning my love for sweet, voluptuous curves, like the ones lining her body.

"So, what are you guys doing here?" Smith's abrupt question pulls my mind from the gutter.

Melanie shifts on her feet, her nervousness obvious. "I brought Melanie by to see the place... To rent."

Liza gasps, leaping to hug Melanie's neck again. "You decided to stay?"

Melanie nods, a laugh bubbling up as Liza wraps her in a hug. Their excited bounces draw the attention of Smith's little princess and she jumps in her chair, mimicking the women with a Velociraptor shriek.

"Wow, Fifi!" Smith scoops his daughter up, who slaps her dad's rough cheeks between those chubby little fingers. He beams and I have to look away, so the room doesn't read my jealousy. Smith deserves it all. Truthfully, he should have had this life ages ago. I just wish we were doing this side by side... raising our kids together.

"Come on. Let me show you around." Liza tugs Melanie, hauling the woman toward the bedroom by the elbow, as she rambles excitedly. "The ladies downstairs are cool. They leave you alone, mostly, but sometimes the perm stank floats upstairs. Have lots of candles on hand."

Melanie chuckles, and the husky sound fires straight at my balls as I watch them both walk away.

"Dude, you got it bad."

Smith jerks me out of my Melanie-induced trance. "Shut it, man." Out of self-preservation, I turn to pack the open box by Smith's entertainment center. "You almost ready for the move?" His shelves are nearly bare: a stack of paperbacks, a few blue rays, and frames of our earlier days.

I mean... he barely rented the place for three months.

Normally, moving in with a girlfriend so fast is stupid, but Smith and Liza have been in love since they learned two plus two.

When he doesn't answer, I risk a glance at my buddy. He and his daughter have matching grins. "You gonna tell me how this little... run in happened? You out searching for tenants for my place?"

The tips of my ears burn. "Random chance. I stopped to get a coffee on the way here. She had old man Leary's listing. A. B. C. Here we are."

"Mmm, hmm."

"You want help with these boxes or not?" I ask, giving Smith a *shut-the-fuck-up* look as the girls' voices move closer. "I don't want Melanie thinking we're talking about her out here. She's already as skittish as a kitten on an alligator farm."

"Let me show you the kitchen. Smith hates it, but he's spoiled at *Two-Fourteen*." Liza rolls her eyes, causing Melanie to chuckle and Smith to wink when she looks his way.

I shake my head. "You guys are too much."

Smith glances toward the women and falls quiet. "I'll leave you alone, man. Just saying… she's a sweet girl. She deserves someone like you."

I nod, keeping my mouth shut. I'm dying to ask about Melanie's situation, but I want the info from her. I wanna earn it.

From what I've heard around town, these past few weeks have been hell. The pain is clear as day in her eyes.

I want to erase it.

Having her this close to the hardware store makes things easier. The apartment over Klassy Kuts is on my way into town, close to the diner, steps from the shops. If Melanie takes this place, we're guaranteed to cross paths. She's been elusive since the festival when I first saw those wild curls flying free from a holiday scarf. Those sweet green eyes drove me crazy, so sad in the middle of laughing families and twinkling lights. They ate at me.

But she wasn't there with me, and I had no idea who the curvy bombshell was at the time. Only that the douche yelling at her in the middle of the sidewalk didn't deserve her. The jackass is lucky I didn't rip his throat out.

Since their wedding fell through, now's my chance.

Anticipation speeds my movements. I've got the rest of Smith's shelf packed before the girls' chatter interrupts the hamster wheel of ideas rolling in my head.

"When is the place available?" Melanie asks, following Liza back into the living area.

"How quick can you move in?" Smith asks, placing Fiona back in her exersaucer. He passes her a folder from his desk in the corner. "This is my lease, and the house rules from the landlord. Kitty's leaving it up to me to find a sublet."

She takes the file but doesn't open it. "I'm sure whatever rules won't be a problem. I don't have any pets. Parties aren't an issue."

"Not throwing ragers every weekend?" I ask, unable to stop myself from digging a little deeper.

Sharp emeralds cut into me before turning back to Smith with a smile. "You don't have to worry about ragers or anything else. It's just me. I work from home and have no life." The lilt in Melanie's voice belies the sarcasm.

I smile. "Stay in this town long and the biddies will take over your social calendar."

"Whether you want them to or not." Liza chuckles and Smith snorts.

"Watch out for Betsy. She's all hands. Kitty gets a little pushy at times too. The landlord working below you can be difficult sometimes."

"Oh, honey. I think you're the only tenant Kitty pestered. She couldn't care less about her tenant's work schedule or their dinner menu." Liza's smirk softens her tease as Smith's cheeks pink under his tan skin.

"Leave me alone, woman. I never flirted back." Liza wraps her arms around his waist and squeezes. Smith rolls his eyes, pretending to be put out while he focuses on Melanie. "Anyway... do you have questions about the place? It's not much. But the furniture comes with." Smith looks around and frowns. "That's not great, either. The stuff is a little run down, but rent's cheap and Kitty will let you do whatever you want in here... paint-wise. Probably anything else, too."

Melanie scans the living area, biting the corner of her lip. I try to see it through her eyes: dingy paint, dusty moldings—thank you, Smith. I know for a fact, the bathroom door sticks when it's cold out. Not exactly a sparkly oasis for a woman.

I tape down my box and catch Melanie's nervous stare. "I can help fix anything you need here. Paint. Whatever you want." The offer is out of my mouth before I think about how eager it sounds.

Smith's eyes dance. "Tyler's very good with his hands—oomph."

Liza's elbow in Smith's ribcage cuts off the rest of the insinuation. Her apologetic smile soothes the blush creeping into Melanie's face. "We'll have his stuff cleared in no time, so whenever you need to move is fine. The pots and pans were Kitt's but we can pack those up for you if you have your own stuff."

Melanie nods.

Liza peeks my way. "Tyler really is the best with anything you need fixed up. He's working on our house right now." She gazes lovingly at Smith... *I'm not the least bit jealous.* "He's got plenty of experience." Liza's lips snap closed, curling in on themselves, as if catching the possible double meaning.

"Guys...what the hell!" I glare at them both and turn to face Melanie, hoping she's capable of looking me in the eye after my friends' pushiness.

"I'm sorry about those two. They've been hanging around the biddies in town too long. But I am more than happy to help with whatever you need... after you get settled. Or before. I can help move anything you need."

Melanie opens her mouth, then snaps it closed, taking in the three of us with raised brows. I feel like a freaking overeager idiot. "Uh..."

"Take your time," I rush. "I'll load some boxes in the truck and drive you back to your car whenever y'all are done."

I grab the box at my side before I can embarrass myself more and head for the stairs. Conversation picks up the moment the latch catches, leaving me conflicted. Part of me loves how nervous Melanie seems around me, all blushing and tongue tied. The other part wants her to chill out, open up, and go to dinner with me.

Something about her, though, since that first night I saw her sadness, calls for me to fix her pain.

I just need to figure out her combination.

Chapter Four

♥

*W*hat the hell am I doing here?

It's probably the fifth time I've asked myself the same question since leaving home. So far, my only excuse is to follow up on the repairs I offered last week. Just will she buy it?

I look down at my empty hands. "I should have at least brought a coffee." It's the great equalizer and my dumbass has nothing.

Still, the tiny ounce of common sense in my head loses its battle, and I lift a fist, rapping out a corny beat. The end of the tune hangs in the air. I can't help it. It's too damn fun. A smile spreads across my face, lightening my mood, until the cheap wood door rips from under my hand, an angry-looking pixie standing in its place.

"I hate when people do tha—What the hell are you doing here?"

Isn't that the million-dollar question?

"Checking in. Seeing if you need anything. Other than cleaning Smith's man-gunk. I'm not doing that."

A shocked tinkle of laughter fills the small space. "Man-gunk? Seriously?"

Melanie's green eyes sparkle, the yellow flecks around her pupils giving them a feline quality... They're beautiful.

A raucous noise below overtakes the quiet space upstairs and Melanie shakes her head. "You wanna come in? They've been at it all morning," she says, when the hen party below becomes too loud to talk over.

"Sure." I follow the swish of Melanie's hips, chuckling when she rushes to tuck something behind a couch pillow. My curiosity piques, but I keep my mouth shut in favor of not getting myself kicked out within minutes of walking in.

Inside, she scrambles to clear a few items off the coffee table.

"You don't have to clean up for me." I turn away out of pure self-preservation as Melanie bends over with those drool-inducing yoga pants melted to her ass. My heart rate kicking up is a glaring reminder of my current—long—dry spell.

Squatting down, she lifts a box from the chair that a lady left behind two tenants ago. *God! Those curves.*

Turning, I discreetly adjust myself. Maybe I should have called... okay, gotten her number, then called. Then, she wouldn't be torturing me by bending over to clean with that baggy sweater falling off her shoulder. I might as well have fucking x-ray vision for how it cups her figure in all the best places.

"Sorry… I-I didn't expect company." Melanie turns before I can school my expression into something more respectful than horny pre-teen.

"I've seen worse." I smile, hoping to ease her worry. She pauses the television, freezing the image on a dolled-up couple holding hands over some artfully designed dinner in the middle of the desert. I point at the screen, confused. "What the hell is that?"

Melanie chuckles, pride lighting her heart-shaped face. Those jade eyes sparkle as her confidence blooms right in front of me. "Guilty pleasure… reality T.V." She shrugs. "Gotta do something while I unpack."

Boxes line the wall, but they're stacked neatly inside the living room, not cluttering every square foot like when I helped Smith move just a week ago. Lace curtains billow in the window and there are candles sitting in little holders across the room.

I step into the living room, now that it meets 'company standards'. "How have you done this much in a week?"

She looks around. "There's still a lot to do, but so far, no complaints. Can I get you a water?"

"Uh, sure. Thanks." She stops at the fridge while I take a seat on one end of the hand-me-down couch. "Did you talk to Kitty?" I ask when she passes me the water.

Melanie's expression softens. "She's great." She falls into the armchair closest to me. "Gave me carte blanche to create my palace."

"Good." I lean back, stretching my arm across the pillows as Melanie's lips wrap around her plastic bottle. "Anything you need help with?" Her eyes cut my way over her bottle and my ears heat. *Shit.* My fingers tug at my too-long hair, trying to hide my body's response to this woman as she slides forward in the chair and rests her water on the table.

She looks like a queen, perched on the edge of her throne, as she studies my presence. "Why are you here?"

I lean forward, resting my elbows on my knees. "Checking in. Like I said." I shrug, pretending I haven't thought about her every second of the past week. "Smith didn't have time to do a thing when he lived here. I figured the place isn't quite up to snuff."

"Up to snuff?" She crinkles her nose.

Oh, good lord. Why can't I talk to this woman without feeling like I'm back in high school asking out the head cheerleader?

What the hell's wrong with me? I've charged compounds with fewer nerves than I have sitting in front of one gorgeous woman.

"You said something before about painting." My face flushes, and I chug half my water to hide it. She's quiet. The room is quiet. Peeling the label off my bottle stops my ass from shifting uncomfortably on the couch, but not my much.

Finally, she snorts, falling back in the chair. "Yeah. Carte blanche, remember? I'm going to throw color all over this place."

The tightness in my chest eases, and I grin. "Gaining inspiration?" I ask, quirking a brow at her hot pink tights and tie-dye sweater.

She looks down, an adorable flush darkening her cheeks. "Maybe... You got an issue with a little fun?" She stands suddenly and heads for the hallway, and I'm left staring at her sexy backside, wondering what the hell just happened.

My feet kick into high gear as her voice trails away, mumbling about freedom, and fun, and *terd* men. I cock my head at her back. "Excuse me... Did you just say terd men?" My laughter bounces off the walls, startling the pissed off tigress, who realizes I'm on her tail.

She flips, fists digging into her hips and I can't help but grin at her put out expression.

I stop. "So, am I the terd man? Or someone else?"

"I don't know you," she says, her voice pitching. "Not well enough to know if you're a terd." She huffs, blowing a piece of bang out of her face in frustration. "I'm just tired of... of... giving into other people's opinions. And I'm done with blah-beige and boring-black."

"You shouldn't give into other people's opinions."

"Damn right!" Confusion darkens her eyes as she scans my face.

I wait, feeling wholly out-of-place having to win over someone in this small town. Everyone knows everyone here. Not a single woman in this town doesn't know my dating history, my family history, and every goddamn thing else in my life.

I guess she finds whatever validation she needs to drop the stiff shoulder. "Sorry. I didn't mean to pop your head off."

"No worries. We're good."

Nodding awkwardly, she turns, leaving me to follow with my hands in my pockets. She stops in front of a row of familiar paint samples.

Dad insisted his small-town hardware store differ from big box stores, all the way down to our custom printed paint samples. Free estimates. Classes. He offers coffee in the front window for customers, truly horrible coffee, but still. Dad prioritizing customers keeps them coming back two decades later.

I stand behind her. "You pick one yet?"

"Debating between these for the living." She snatches four, barely distinguishable pale yellows and three hues of blue with varying brightness from their tape on the wall. I grab the two coral shades and follow her back to the coffee table, where she straightens the colors to compare.

I fight a smile at the excitement dancing across her face.

"They all seem good. But why so many?"

"Why not?" Her lips purse. The weight of that question feels more than surface level, but I focus on the swatches, not the suspicion darkening those green irises.

"No problem with choices, except having to make one." I tap on the gray closest to me. "This is our big seller after that Reno T.V. show made it popular."

"Dammit! See. Now, I don't want it." I chuckle as she slaps all the *trendy grays* off the coffee table. "Next." She pulls the corals forward. "My bedroom."

I lift them to her face, pretending to evaluate any damn thing except her perfectly upturned pout. One brow arches as I turn the lighter color next to her cheek. "This one is that calm front you show the world, the lady in the streets, if you will." I grin and set it upside down on the table. Next, my preference. Our eyes lock.

"This... is the freak in the sheets." I wink and Melanie snatches the sample, her cheeks pinking through a playful scowl.

"I assume that one's your preference."

She wants me to deny that?

I chuckle. "No smart man should tell his woman who to be." That snaps those plump lips shut and I lean in, laying both colors side by side in her lap, leaving my hands on her thighs, holding them in place. She blinks.

"I prefer my woman to be a swirl of each." I point at the subdued sample. "A soft spot for me to relax." Then to the accent color. "With a wild side, she saves just for me."

Melanie's throat bobs, a light rosy hue darkening her olive skin. "Got a virgin obsession?"

"Not necessarily. Don't care how much experience anyone has, as long as they happily consented and enjoyed themselves. My goal is for *my woman* to know she's safe to express whatever she wants in that bedroom. With me."

Heat sparks in the air between us.

"I could help you paint, accent wall or not."

"Why would you do that?" she asks, suspicion lacing the question.

My smile grows. "Why not?" I wait for the smack that comes a few seconds after I turn Melanie's words back on her.

"I'm sure you have other things to do. Aren't you remodeling Smith and Liza's right now?"

"I am.

"So, why would you take on my crap? I can roll a paintbrush."

What's the best way to answer that without sounding creepy?

"Well, for one, you don't roll a paintbrush, so now I *know* I need to be here. Two... It's a small town." I shrug. "People do things for each other."

My phone vibrates in my pocket, reminding me that I'm needed at the store so Dad can run errands. "Speaking of..." I grab the colors she's picked so far. "I'm managing the store this afternoon. How about I pick up a few gallons and drop them off after my shift?"

Melanie is off the couch, arms crossed, before I can blink. Her face is a beautiful mask of confusion, brows drawn together, mouth slightly ajar.

I stand, our bodies separated by tension-filled inches. Reaching out, I pressed a finger under her chin to close her dropped jaw.

"What's up, gorgeous? Can't a guy offer to be nice without setting off alarms?"

She scoffs. "Not in my experience."

Ignoring that, I smile, holding out my hand. "Have you decided on the vibe of your bedroom?"

"Both." That mischievous smirk as she snaps the two vibrant colors in my hand shoots the blood straight to my groin. A condition that worsens when she catches the tip of her tongue between her teeth, giving me a peek that drives every thought into naughty territory.

I close my fingers over hers, maintaining contact. "I'll be back... with paint... and dinner." To seal the deal, I break out my dimpled smile, banking on the fact that it never fails to win a date.

Before anymore sass comes out of that pouty mouth, I head for the door. "See you in a few hours, gorgeous."

Melanie's wide emerald eyes spark with challenge. Wisely, she bites her tongue. My returning works in her favor, anyway. She'd chew off her own foot to decline the offer of free help.

With a final wink, I pull the door closed behind me, packing away the image of Melanie's flushed cheeks and ample curves waiting for me to the back of my mind. It's the only way I'll survive the next few hours at work.

Tonight, when I'm home in my little fixer upper—alone—I'll unpack that one in the shower like a grown ass man.

Chapter Five

Melanie

The moment the door clicks in place, I lunge for my phone. Luckily, I saved Liza's number in here the night we met. We were the only two tomatoes sitting front row at an all-male revue. Our mutual embarrassment forged a bond I am extremely thankful for now. At the time, I was relieved to have another woman at my bachelorette party not having a conniption to touch naked torsos and thrusting pelvises. Hello… random dude's man sweat. No, thank you.

With the phone and my ear, I bend to pick up my discarded samples, stacking them in the corner neatly before taking our empty water bottles to the recycle bin. "Come on, Liza, pick up."

Energy pumps through my limbs until I'm bopping on my toes with every ring. I wish there was something left for me to clean in here. Unpacking is fine, but my hands itch to scrub something.

Finally, Liza's breathless voice answers the phone, just as I'm about to hang up. "Hey, girlie!"

"Hey! Did I interrupt something? You sound like you sprinted to the phone." A rumble of laughter fills the background, followed by a slap, and Liza's flustered giggle. "Oh... hey, I did interrupt something. I can let you go."

"No, no, I can talk. Smith, stop it." A door closes on the background noise and Liza sighs. "Sorry, I'm here. How's it going?"

"Good. Great, actually. Unpacking is a pain. You know how that is. Umm..." I'm not sure how to start. Or what I even want to say, ask. "So, uh, I had a visitor." Turning, I go for the coffee carafe, needing my hands busy to focus my brain.

"Don't tell me Aaron is trying to win you back."

"What? No!" My screech bounces off the kitchen walls and I nearly drop this morning's coffee pot as I scrub it for tomorrow. "That twatopotamus is never getting into my house." The very idea irritates the hell out of me. I scrub harder, my knuckles knocking inside the glass. "Hopefully, he knows better."

She snorts. "If he tries, let Smith know. Bet he'd make some yummy *Goodbye Earl* soup."

"Aww, you're such a sweety." We both giggle like middle schoolers gossiping, and I finish setting the automatic timer on my cheapo machine.

In the living room, I lift my last box and set it on my desk to unpack. Yesterday, I bought a new lavender bookshelf from one of the downtown stores. Tiny crescent moons and hand-painted stars decorate the pale wood. It's unique enough to accent the original furniture and small enough to fit in the nook beside Kit's black T.V. stand.

"So, who visited?" Liza asks, snapping me from my task. "Do you need us to come over?"

"Tyler stopped by," I blurt before I can talk myself out of it.

"Oh...?" I stop at the lilt in her voice, a stack of bare-chested paperbacks in my hand freezing inches from their shelf home. "Are you guys hanging out?"

"*No!*" Heat rushes to my face and I fan myself, despite no one here to witness my embarrassment. "I'm still getting out of Aaron's mess. I don't need another guy hanging around."

"Is your mother-in-law still giving you problems?"

I scoff. "She was never my mother-in-law!"

"Thank God for that!"

"Right!" The idea that I'd be stuck with that woman the rest of my life is almost worse than being stuck with her son. They're a toss-up. "She's up my ass to get the *two* boxes I left in her garage."

"What the hell?"

I shake my head—not that Liza can see me—and finish stacking the tiny, bronzed puppies my grandmother collected as bookends. They're too adorable beside those big hulking chests, but perfect to keep the book covers smooshed together. I can't have visitors seeing my romance-obsessed guilty pleasure.

"It's all good. After this, I never have to see her again. I just need a truck big enough for two giant wardrobe boxes, or I'll have to let her trash my work suits and pretty shoes."

The condescending memory of Aaron telling me I wouldn't need to worry about work after the wedding triggers the same anger that I felt that day. Not because he cared to support me taking care of the home, or our future children. No, he said my wardrobe wasn't to country club standards, and didn't fit with his mother's beneficiary dinners and charitable galas.

I bite back a growl, slamming my copy of Pride and Prejudice on the shelf with too much umph.

"You okay?" Liza's voice is thick with concern as I drag in a deep breath. Those memories are why I should avoid the hyper-friendly boy next door.

"I'm fine…"

"Okay, then. Back to Tyler. You know he isn't just some guy, right? He's a really good guy, Mel. A rare one."

"But why's he hanging around me?"

"Why wouldn't he?"

"That's what he said." I frown, giving up on my decorating endeavor in favor of the couch.

"Sounds like Tyler's a smart man."

I'm getting nowhere.

Just then, baby Fiona bellows in the distance, followed by Smith's slightly panicked shout. "One sec." The sound of Liza entering her house increases the cacophony of noise. "Aww, baby girl. You didn't like your snack?" I can't hear Smith's response, but his pleading does *not* soothe Fiona's cries.

"I'll let you go." Liza is too close to Tyler to understand my hesitation, anyway.

"It's okay. Fifi objects to Smith's new baby food recipe." Her laughter is full of joy and love. I close my eyes, shoving down the jealousy that springs up where it belongs.

"Has Smith thought of starting his own baby food line? Markets go crazy for local vendors. Every store from here to Lexington would be all over the military hero turned baby food maker. The ads practically write themselves."

She chuckles. "Hmm, maybe. I'll talk to him about it." Rustling static fills the phone and then Liza's sweet voice. "I got you, baby. Let's get cleaned up." There's a pause and I assume she picked up a food covered Fiona. "Sorry for the chaos, Mel. We got a call that the lawyer could fit us in this afternoon about the adoption, so woke up this little princess, and she hasn't stopped punishing us since."

"*Hah!* I'd be cranky if you woke me up, too."

"I know. I know. Not smart. But we've gotta get to Mr. Boyd's office before he leaves for the weekend. We've got a few questions about finalizing Fi's papers and want to make sure we crossed all our Ts."

"I get it. She's very lucky to have you, Liza." My empty apartment is a stark contrast to the life on the other end of the phone. "Look, I'll let you go. Good luck this afternoon."

"Thanks. I'll call you tomorrow. Well, I'll text... in case you're otherwise occupied."

"*Liza!*"

"Oh, give him a chance, girl. You cut the loser. Now, reward yourself with real man."

I scoff, but my lady parts agree with Liza, not my anti-man policy.

Those muscles busting out of Tyler's tight work shirts say trouble, but the soft puppy dog eyes soften my resolve. They make Tyler more approachable... or at least, less kick-him-in-the-crotchable.

Now, with Liza's tease rolling around in my head, the temptation tingling low in my belly is dangerous. How the hell am I going to keep my resolve if the man really does stop by after work?

"I knew it."

Frustrated, I break down another empty box and prop it behind my recycling bin. I need something to busy my hands. The later it gets, the less I believe Tyler will stop by. Not that I'm watching the clock. He's only dropping off paint. Who cares when he does it? I'll pay him, say thank you, and send him on his way.

I glance around the kitchen. There's nothing left to clean, dammit. I've unpacked the few boxes I hauled over from storage this afternoon. Plates and cups, cutlery and the cookbooks I found at a going out of business sale in college. Never got to use them, but maybe now, I'll have time.

My stomach growls. Unfortunately, the one thing I haven't had time for is stocking the fridge. Disappointment sits heavy on my chest, but there's no use in digging into the fact that I might have looked forward to tonight more than I admitted.

Resigned, I pull down my favorite bowl, the blue one with the *Ghost Hunters* logo, and pour it full of honey nut cereal. At least when I'm down, these tiny freedoms, like eating the cereal I want and not Aaron's sugary box with a child's toy at the bottom. However, it's hard not to beat myself up for staying with that over-grown man-child.

So much wasted time!

A knock sounds as I grab my bowl to eat in front of my over-crowded DVR. *"Ugh!"* Sitting my promised dinner on the counter, I open the door without checking who it is.

"Hi there," Tyler says, beaming. A paper sack balances on his hip, while he somehow squeezes the handles of three gallons of paint in the fist at his side.

My mouth drops. "What are you doing here?"

One dark eyebrow lifts over those big brown eyes, the dangerous ones made hotter by the challenge dancing inside them. "I told you I'd be back after work." He holds the bag that spells suspiciously like hamburgers out for me to carry, and I snap out of my stupor.

"Sorry... here." I take the bag and set it on my tiny dinette in the corner while Tyler sets the cans on my countertop with a grunt. He flexes his thick fingers, stretching out the muscles after carrying everything in one go.

"I picked up burgers from the diner since Smith is off today. I hope you don't mind cheese. Minnie put all the fixins on the side, so you can make it how you like."

My throat closes up as I pull out the Styrofoam cartons. Aaron never cared about my preference, nor what I wanted for dinner. He would have brought me a salad, in deference to the extra cushion he told me I needed to lose. If I got lucky, he'd add chicken.

My heart drops when I pop the top of a side salad until Tyler walks up behind me. "Here." He passes me a plain burger, ready to build to my preference, just like he said. "I wasn't sure what sides you liked. I got a bit of everything." A muscular arm reaches around me and opens a container of curly fries, and another with mac n' cheese. He keeps pulling... sweet potato mash, green beans, and fried okra.

"Good lord, how hungry are you?" I ask incredulously. My worry over the side salad washes away with the enticing scents of down-home diner food spread across my table.

To my surprise, a dusty rose hue spreads across his cheeks as he shrugs. "Sorry. I, uh, I didn't know what you like." He pulls out two more see-through containers with slices of pie and my mouth falls open. Guess he's not all that concerned about my healthy eating and cutting calories.

Needing space from the masculine soap wafting off Tyler, I turn around and grab plates for our mountain of food. "You want a beer? Water?"

"Either's fine."

Tyler takes a seat, his massive frame dwarfing the space at the tiny table. I set both bottles in front of his plate and sit to unpack my burger and dress it how I like. He passes me the curly fries and I smile, scooping a handful before spooning a few fried okras, as well. For once, I completely ignore the tasteless salad I've eaten all too often.

Warmth spreads through my chest, easing some of the embarrassment I normally feel eating in front of a stranger. A sexy stranger.

"You didn't have to do all this," I say, topping my burger with a small amount of ketchup. The last thing I want is to look like a pig in front of Tyler when it squishes out of the bottom the way I prefer.

He shrugs, biting his fully layered burger without a lick of awkwardness. "We both gotta eat, right? Sorry, I was late though. I grabbed Mr. Blackburn's dinner and dropped it off on the way over here."

I stop chewing. "Smith's dad?"

He nods, as if taking an elderly man dinner is no big deal. "Smith has an appointment with a family lawyer, so I wanted to check in on him, anyway."

"That's really nice of you." A soft pink darkens his winter tan at my compliment, but I dig into my food to not embarrass him more.

Tonight's dinner may be totally out of left field, but Tyler is a friend of a friend, and obviously a nice guy if he's taking a sick old man dinner. I shouldn't be nervous. This is a favor, and a shared meal, not a date.

"So... your dad owns the hardware store, right?"

"Yeah, he's stepped back a lot, but it's his baby."

I glance at the counter. "How often do you deliver paint to your customers?"

Tyler's face freezes mid-shew, and he coughs, almost choking on a bite of burger. He downs half his water bottle to clear the windpipe and wipes his mouth. "Occasionally," he says roughly. "I mean, if I'm doing repairs, I'll pick up supplies on the way."

"But you aren't doing repairs here..."

"I offered to help paint," he says, so matter of fact that I just stare.

"I didn't take you up on it."

Tyler's sinful smirk is a straight challenge. "You didn't refuse, either." *Cocky shit.* "You really sending me home after I eat a big dinner? What if my tummy gets upset for not waiting thirty minutes to drive? I could cramp up."

I shake my head, laughing. "You're an idiot."

"Never denied that." His self-satisfied smile doesn't annoy me like Aaron's used to. Tyler's is less smug... more playful, and it puts me at ease to enjoy our meal.

The good-natured ribbing lasts the rest of our meal. Tyler shares his funniest homeowner-attempted repairs and the stupidest things he's had to fix. I share the most ridiculous things Aaron would call his mother for... like how to stain remove chocolate ice cream, or how long to boil pasta.

"Was he at least good in bed?" he asks, finishing off the last bite of his pie.

"*Hah!*" A very unladylike snort spurts water out of my nose. "Oh my god!" Heat rushes my face as Tyler cracks up, rushing to hand me extra napkins. I wipe the wetness off my face and the front of my shirt, not meeting his eye.

"Well, that answers that." He bundles up our trash and Styrofoam containers into the to-go bags and sets them by the door.

When the tiny table is clean, Tyler leans against the kitchen door frame, arms crossed over that impressive chest. His dumbfounded expression nails me in place, making me feel entirely too vulnerable under his stare. "I have to ask… why were you marrying him then?"

My spine stiffens, and I turn, giving myself a break from that sculpted body. Especially when talking about my failed relationship. I take a second beer from the fridge for Tyler, and one for myself, before meeting his eyes. Nothing but patience reflects back, but admitting failure is hard.

I glance away, unwilling to risk judgment from the Adonis god in my apartment. "Isn't that the magic question?"

Hell, I have no idea why I put up with Aaron for so long.

Sighing, I pass Tyler his beer, focusing on those long fingers grip the bottle. His other hand finds my wrist, holding me in place. "Look at me."

I don't.

My eyes fix on where his calloused grip wraps across my smooth skin. Tyler isn't having it. "Listen." He tips my chin, forcing me to face his sincerity. "He didn't deserve you."

"How do you know that?" My voice lodges in my throat and I swallow. "I could be a raging bitch, for all you know."

That earns me a smile. "You're sassy, but sass is hot." His dimple pops out as he looks up in the air, tilting his head back and forth as if weighing something. Finally, he shakes his head. "Nope... my bitch-o-meter has nothing."

My bark of laughter surprises even me, but he joins in. Jerking my chin free, I swat at the set of granite abs a few inches away before pulling back. "Good lord," I mumble, shaking out my hand.

Tyler chuckles, seemingly pleased that I notice the effects of what must be significant workouts.

To hide my embarrassment—and my tomato face—I collect my purse from the hook by the door.

"What are you doing?"

"Paying you." My brain works through the calculation for the high-end paint buckets, the one-coat, primer included, out of my price range kind. Easy enough... I reach for the plastic bag Tyler brought, pulling out a receipt for the rolls of edging tape, brushes, and roller sponges. "Man, you went all out!"

Tyler chuckles. "I don't do anything halfway, baby."

I cut my eyes to the side, catching Tyler's smirk. "Har. Har. Says every man ever."

These supplies are pricier than I would buy myself. Nevertheless, I count out enough money to pay Tyler back for his kindness and at least a portion of dinner. Checking another area, I hide bills; I don't notice Tyler stalk closer until he's at my side.

"Again, what are you doing?"

"Paying you. What does it look like?"

"I never asked for payment. I offered to bring supplies over after work."

Slamming my wallet closed, I frown at the six-foot stack of muscle standing way too close. "Don't you not want to get paid?"

He straightens. "No, not really."

My arms fall. "Why the hell not?"

One shoulder lifts. "I didn't itemize an invoice. I offered to help. Haven't you ever had a painting party? Food. Drinks. Holey clothes you're willing to destroy."

I glance at the ironed polo stretching across Tyler's thick chest, down to the worn leather belt holding up his clean, dark denim. They hug every sexy contour of those thick thighs, but don't for a second pass for painting clothes. "You planning to paint in those?"

Tyler grins, his toothpaste commercial smile blinding my common sense. "There's plenty to do before painting, sassy pants. That's what the other bag is for." Reaching across me, Tyler grabs a roll of painter's tape and waves it in the air. "We got work to do tonight."

"We?"

Without answering, Tyler grabs the plastic bag and walks to the back of my apartment. He stops right outside my bedroom with an expectant look. "I assume you want to start in the bedroom..."

"Wait!" I rush after him, but Tyler's faster and opens my door before I can stop him.

"What the—?" Tyler's mouth hangs open as he stares inside my room, shocked.

Rushing, I cross the living room and slap at his arm just before he walks into my mess. Boxes and clothes cover every available flat surface. My bed is neat, but shoes litter underneath like little ants marching to their dust bunny death. I haven't had time to drive thirty minutes to the bigger stores for organizers and shoe racks.

And since I'm not quick enough, Tyler gets the Full Monty view before turning his cheesy grin on me. Happiness dances in his eyes. Pieces of floppy hair fall across his forehead, bopping as Tyler hums the theme to Sanford & Sons, growing louder and louder.

Pulling that enormous body away is impossible, so I move to block the doorway instead, praying my glare burns a hole right through that smugly handsome face. "No one invited you in my bedroom."

The rest of the apartment is spick and span and he had to come in here!

"You sure that's a bedroom? Looks like a back wood flea market to me."

Huffing, I toss my hands to the side. "There is no storage in this place! Sue me."

Tyler wisely keeps further comments to himself as he nudges past me into my not-quite-so-tidy sanctuary. "You're saying we need a date to The Container Store?"

"What! No!" I rush behind Tyler, who's already unpacking brushes and trim tape on my bed.

With his back turned, I slide a stack of bras into an open box beside the curio cabinet in the corner. At least most of the stuff sitting out is more lack of space issue than embarrassment.

Honestly, hitting one of the home stores would help maximize the tiny space. Not that I want Tyler searching for under bed storage and underwear dividers with me. That's just ridiculous.

Tyler stands back, waving at our tools spread out on my bed. He obviously came prepared to work. Mentally, I'm at the point of 'buy paint samples'. Adding color to my life post-breakup seemed like a no brainer. Like taking back part of myself I buried to fit into that stodgy black and white world.

When I don't make a move, Tyler tosses me a roll of painter's tape, smiling. "I'm just glad to see you're not entirely perfect." He shivers. "The rest of your apartment scared me."

"Shut up!"

His laughter bounces off my walls, making it impossible to stay annoyed. He moves to the large dresser and grips the end, man-handling it easily off the wall. I stare, too fixated on the biceps stretching the fabric of that polo to be useful.

"If it makes you nervous, we can talk about a second date later. Why don't you tape the trim and I'll move furniture off the wall so we're ready for tomorrow?"

I snort at the assumption of a second date, but inside, my belly flip flops with anticipation.

In no time, he has the dresser, curio, my end table and bed frame a few feet from the wall, and I've taped the trim around the door and half the room's baseboards. In the first few minutes of work, I realized I needed a dust rag to guide ahead of my blue tape, otherwise the months of buildup acted as Teflon for the glue.

"Wow! Nice work!" Tyler surveys my progress when I stand, stretching the painful ache in my back.

I wait for whatever criticism or advice the 'professional' plans to give on how to do the job better.

Nothing comes.

Tyler's round eyes scan my chaotic room, calculating. Seeing the results of a productive evening boosts my energy. Although Tyler's sweat-soaked shirt plastered to the deep ridges sculpting that gorgeous chest goes a long way, too. It's hard not to gawk—and drool—but the mess around us is a little more than I can take. If I'm going to get any sleep tonight, I should usher Tyler out so I can finish taping the room.

"We probably should call it for now," he says, reading my mind. "I don't want you breathing paint fumes all night. You got plans tomorrow morning?"

I don't, but I shouldn't admit my exciting weekend includes writing a business plan and applying for every small business loan I can find. Vegging on takeout is a high possibility, and watching trash T.V.

"I guess I'll be painting my bedroom," I say instead.

Tyler grins. "Then I'll be back in the morning."

"No!" My voice goes shrill, and I slap my hand over my mouth, catching my words before more rudeness slips out. "I just mean, you've done enough. You don't want to spend your weekend doing more work."

Tyler's heated gaze scans me up and down. "I can decide how to spend my weekend. I don't think a day with a gorgeous woman sounds like a hardship."

"Shush..." I roll my eyes and head for the door. "Come on, smooth talker. I don't need false flattery."

"False? Honey, I don't do fake anything."

I ignore the put-out expression on his handsome face and stride for the front door. Tyler is hot on my heels, his heavy footsteps echoing in the short hallway. In the kitchen, he grabs my elbow, pulling me around to a stop.

"Do you *mind* if I come back tomorrow to help you paint?"

My lips snap shut. He's asking permission? A guy who looks like Tyler gets his way most of the time. But his brown eyes show nothing but earnest in the question. No expectation, just a little bit of... hope?

"I appreciate it. I just... I don't get why you'd want to."

A small smile tilts those sexy lips. "I told you. A day with a beautiful woman... worth it."

Laughing, I shake my head. "You're as stubborn as a mule, aren't you?"

"Better believe it. Strong as one, too." Tyler flexes, cheesing ear to ear as he bounces in front of me, kissing each bicep like a corny teenager. Total peacock.

"Stop!" I smack that impressive arm, biting back a smile. Flirting with Tyler flutters little butterflies in my belly, but I need space. "Get out of here, you idiot." Tyler's feet dance as I brace my palms against his tree trunk of a torso and push toward the door.

"Okay. Okay. I'll go." Tyler spins, his hands held in the air in faux innocence that I don't believe for a second.

My hands linger on his lower back, playfully urging Tyler closer to the door. He lets me all the way until his hand reaches the door handle and then he turns so fast, I almost slam into his front at the sudden stop.

"Umph!" Quickly, I step back, my face burning under Tyler's knowing smirk.

He runs a finger under my chin, stealing my breath as he lifts, locking me in that fiery gaze. "I'll see you tomorrow, beautiful. Bright and early."

I swallow against the light in those brown eyes.

He's perfection. Usually when guys are this forward, it's a one and done, wham bam, thank you ma'am. It has been a long time since I had a non-self-induced orgasm. I might allow it. Aaron certainly couldn't get the job done. But judging by the passion sizzling off Tyler like a live wire, he would have no problem completing the task.

Am I ready?

I've never been able to separate love and sex. One last glance at Tyler's sexy-as-hell backside on the way out the door makes me want to try.

Leaning my back against the wood, I know my answer. If there were ever a time in my life to taste temptation, the very lickable man that just walked out would be worth the stomachache.

As long as heartache doesn't come with it.

Chapter Six

Tyler

Mama always said the way to a man's heart was through his stomach. I'm hoping the concept applies to women, too. Bringing Melanie flowers seemed like poking a bull with an electric prod. The last thing I want to do is scare her away with some overly romantic gesture. Food seemed like the easiest path to her good side. The French vanilla wafting from the to-go cups tempts even my under-caffeinated brain and I'm usually a straight black drinker.

A much-needed rush of energy hits the moment I knock on the familiar doorway. It never did when my buddy lived here, but Smith never kept me up at night thinking about his soft skin. I love the guy and all, but his scruffy ass is not my type.

Melanie picks that moment to crack open the door an inch, and I almost swallow my tongue. Her nearly black curls stick out in all directions from the messy bun on top of her head. Pillow marks wrinkle her gorgeous face below squinty eyes. A hot pink cut-off top over fuzzy pink shorty-shorts exposes a mouthwatering amount of Mediterranean olive skin.

My voice sticks in my throat as I try not to stare with every spare blood cell headed south of the border.

"What time is it?" she rasps, looking deliciously rumpled.

"Breakfast time." I hold out the white paper sack, praying she doesn't notice the bulge I'm trying to hide below. "Apple crisps, blueberry muffins, and scone." I shrug. "I wasn't sure what you liked."

Melanie blinks, her gorgeous green eyes seconds from flaying me over the early morning wake up.

Finally, after a few pounding heartbeats, she steps back, opening wide enough to allow entry. She doesn't wait for me to empty my arms before grabbing one of the hot cups I hold in my hand.

"I hope you have good taste in coffee," she says, closing her eyes and sipping our town's best offering. Her moan sends another shot of caffeine to my morning chub and I shift, discreetly tiling away so she doesn't notice.

I lift a brow. "Sleep well?"

She takes another sip, eyes meeting mine over the top of the cup with a new alertness. My fingertips itch to tuck those loose wisps of hair behind her delicate ear. I rub them together, frowning as Melanie covers her exposed waist, her cheeks pinking.

"I did." She nods, tugging at the hem of those tiny shorts. "I should go change."

Before I can argue, she's out of the kitchen, coffee in hand, and I'm left watching that fantastic ass scoot down the hallway. An image to look back on later for sure.

Needing a distraction, I unpack our breakfast on clean plates from her dish strainer and take them to the tiny table with my coffee. Second time in as many days I've sat here with my stomach in my throat.

It's a stark contrast to grabbing a beer in Smith's bare-boned bachelor. Melanie managed to girly this place up within a week.

Color coordinated kitchen towels hang in perfect fold, not Smith's scrunched mess. A decorative spoon holder by the stove matches the overall sunshine theme brightening the room. Cookbooks line the counter, ending with an elaborate metal sunshine figurine. It's a picture of cheerful and vibrant.

Minutes tick by. The longer Melanie takes to change, the more sweat pools in my palms. I wipe them on the thighs of my best-looking pair of work jeans just as the door opens. No way would I show up today in my typical paint-covered cargos. Not for the angel walking my way in another pair of neon leggings and an oversized sweatshirt. All the delicious curves I admired a minute ago hide under baggy fabric and I frown.

"You're going to burn up in that." It's only freezing outside, not inside her cozy apartment.

"I'll be fine." Melanie's eyes close as she sits across from me and takes a long drag of coffee. She picks the apple crisps, so I choose the blueberry muffin—my favorite—and break off the top, the best part. "Thanks for bringing these."

"You're welcome." My chest swells. "I miss the fuzzy jammies, though."

Melanie's face pinks. "Shut up." She smirks, taking a bite of her breakfast while doing her best to not look my way. "I didn't expect you so early."

"For once, my early hours work for my benefit."

She snorts, covering her pinked cheeks like she can hide the cuteness. I rub my thumb across the rough material on my thigh to stop myself from reaching out and stroke that smattering of freckles across her nose.

To distract myself, I focus on the day ahead. "Did you finish taping last night?"

"Mmm."

"Mmm? Is that 'mmm, I did. Or mmm, I fell asleep with sweet dreams of Tyler?"

"*Hah!*" Melanie smacks my arm, and I grin. I love when she touches me... anywhere. Her husky laugh does dangerous things to the amount of blood left in my head. She eyes me curiously. "You're a lot first thing in the morning."

I chuckle, nodding. "That's what my mama said."

Melanie shakes her head, standing up to trash her wrapper and mine. "You sure you want to spend your morning off painting my bedroom?"

I stand, coming up behind Melanie at the sink with our plates. Her breath catches. Carefully, I place them in the sink over her shoulder, breathing in the blueberry notes in her hair. They're sweeter than the muffin I just finished.

"Can't think of anywhere I'd rather be."

Electricity zings as those shimmering green orbs angle up to meet mine. I can't move back. Can't break the spell to grant her space. My eyes fall to where her throat works.

"Okay." The words are just above a whisper, her lips drawn tight.

Her vulnerability calls to me. The urge to protect holds me back from pushing too fast. God knows, every part of me wants to throw this woman over my shoulder and use that bedroom for something other than painting. Or the couch. Or the fucking kitchen counter.

God! It's been too damn long since I felt a pull toward anyone. I thought I was broken.

After returning to the states, risking losing anyone else I loved felt like too much. Because I did love my brothers-in-arms. We protected each other. Relied on each other. The moment I lost one brother in what should have been a routine recognizance mission, part of me shut down. So many of my men needed healing back home, including my lifelong best friend. Smith took more than a beating to his body. I guess I felt like my pain paled in comparison to his scars.

Sucking in a deep breath, I shutter those dark thoughts, and focus on the beauty in front of me. "Why don't I get started with the roller while you finish taping?"

She nods, eyes blown wide as I take a step back. I need a little breathing room before I do something to derail the small amount of trust I've earned so far. She dries her hands on the towel, snatching her travel cup on the way to the bedroom. Yet again, I'm left following like an obedient puppy dog.

What the hell is it about this chick?

For the next few hours, our conversation is somewhat awkward. Stilted. Mostly me asking Melanie about her earlier years. I steer clear of the painful breakup. Smith gave me bare details, since we both hated middle school with her ex-fiancé. He was a douche we'd both love to punch in a kidney.

After so many monotonous hours, though, silence has fallen over the room as Melanie focuses on screwing socket covers back in place.

"So, does your mom like traveling the country?" I ask when I'm nearly done rolling paint over the accent wall.

She sighs. "Yeah. I miss the hell out of her, though. Especially now." Her voice cracks and I glance over. The hunch of her shoulders sags under the weight of recent pain.

"You wanna talk about it?"

Hope flashes momentarily before she tamps it down, masking her feelings behind hard eyes and a weak smile. Those green orbs slay me. Emotions fighting for dominance. Sadness and determination. Wary curiosity.

"Nothing to talk about. Except how badass this apartment is going to look by the time I'm done with it."

"Damn straight!"

She looks at me funny and shakes her head. "I just want a new beginning."

The vulnerability in her voice tugs at me, requiring every ounce of my self-control to not cross this room and pull her into my arms. "What else would you like in your new beginning?"

Melanie straightens, turning to the window we opened for ventilation. She chews her lip. "I gave up everything when I moved here. My job. My apartment. My whole damn life." Frowning, she crosses her arms and rests her butt on the windowsill. "I'll never be that stupid again," she says, the chill in her voice matching the chill blowing through the window.

I cock my head to the side, wishing I could soothe the pain, the distrust staring back at me. "You know you weren't stupid, right? That idiot you were with was stupid. If he didn't appreciate your sacrifice... you, he didn't deserve you."

Propping my roller in the empty pan, I step closer, slowly, not wanting to startle the injured tigress in front of me. "Any man would be lucky to have your devotion." I stop, my chest tightening as that plump lower lip trembles. I reach out, grasping her hand in mine. "He should give that devotion back to you tenfold, Mel. Expect nothing less."

"I don't plan on taking anything, Tyler. Screw love!" Her voice hardens, belying the venom that acts as a shield. A soft smile eases out that I don't fight, even as Melanie narrows her eyes. "Don't laugh at me."

"Never." I shake my head at the absurdity, but Melanie doesn't know me, not well enough. "But you can't give up on love. You can't let that asshole steal one more thing from you." Her back stiffens as if electrocuted, and I lift a brow. "You gonna let him win, Mel?"

If eyes could slay, I'd be six feet under right now.

"I'm not letting him do shit! I just don't feel like being some-body's stomping post anymore. The comments on everything I do, what I wear, my weight..."

I scoff as she trails off. "That's not love. And who the hell would complain about your weight?" My voice hardens at the thought. "Did that asshole?"

Immediately, she looks away, and I know.

Fuck that! A force of nature couldn't keep me away now. Screw going slow. The beautiful, and yes curvy, woman deserves a man to worship those shapely thighs and bubble butt on an altar.

God! I want to be that man.

Stalking closer, every cell of my body stands on high alert. Not sandbox level. But ready for a fight, just the same. Her pain calls on me to fix the frown pinching those delicate features. It won't be easy. The thorns on this one are sharp, her body language screaming back off. Don't touch.

Too bad. Someone needs to erase the damage of that rich prick.

He was bad news back in school, before his family moved to Lexington. Hanging with the mucky mucks at the country clubs gave him a false sense of power. We all laughed when he showed up here as an adult, offering to *foster* our budding growth. *Bullshit*. They just wanted to take credit for this town's hard work.

Our mayor, the business owners, the little matchmaking biddies... *they* grew our town's reputation for love and weddings and happy-ever-afters.

She crosses her arms. "It doesn't matter," she says, pissing me off.

"The hell it doesn't."

Startled, her eyes whip to mine. I reach out to stroke the soft skin of her arm, wishing I could crack the steel armor Melanie wraps around herself.

"No man should disparage his woman."

I let my gaze drift down Melanie's torso, making my appreciation clear. The generous swell under that baggy sweatshirt calls for my hands. My cock swells, thinking about burying my face in the pillowy softness, of leaving beard burns behind after I devour each one.

"Especially not one so beautiful."

"Tyler—" She opens her mouth to argue, but I stop her with a finger to the lips. I let my hands fall to the soft fabric on her shoulders and hold her in place. "You, my friend, need to drop kick that asshole's voice straight out of your head." She blinks those doe eyes, and I can't help myself. I reach for a loose curl, tucking it behind her ear. "Say it."

"Say what?" Her voice cracks, confusion flashing as she scans my face.

Keeping my touch gentle, I swipe a thumb under her chin, lifting. "Say he didn't deserve you. That you're drop dead gorgeous and so are those... mmnh curves." I bite off my growl, loving how her pupils blow wide. Loving the flush spreading across the heart-shaped face in my hands.

A puff of air slips past those soft lips, tickling my chin. "Tyler, you don't even know me." Her voice rises, flustered, and I grin.

"I know Liza wouldn't have a bad person as a friend. I know you're a bombshell I'd worship every single day. Having you in my head would drive me crazy. I'd want to show you off, but also want to punch any man who dared to look." Gently, my thumb rubs across her bottom lip, tugging the plumpness. "I know I've wanted to kiss you since the moment I saw you months ago, and it got worse after talking with you in person."

Melanie's tiny pink tongue darts out to wet her lips, grazing my skin. This close, her fruity scent overpowers the hours of paint fumes, and I bite the inside of my jaw to keep from moaning. I don't want to scare Melanie by going too fast, but I can't stand that she thinks she's less because some bastard hurt her.

Time freezes.

She watches me, watching her, eyes wide and growing larger as I lean in, closing the space slow enough that she can object if she wants.

"You want me to stop?" I pause, waiting for Melanie's decision.

Her breath catches, kicking my heart rate up to marathon level.

I'm about to back up and go home, maybe try again another day after I jack off five times, when a slight shake of her head sends my excitement into tenth gear. I dive in, faster than intended, and our lips collide, firing sparks down my spine to the tips of my fingers.

I swipe against her lower lip, drawing it into my mouth for a nibble. Immediately, she softens, her body falling flush with my front, driving me wild. A whimper escapes Melanie that I capture, muffling it with my moan that moves this simple kiss into dangerous territory.

The urge to lift that luscious ass in my hand and haul the woman against me wars with my common sense. Especially when her lips part on a gasp and let me in, our tongues dancing, testing. She's no longer tentative. Her hands roam my chest, my biceps, squeezing, pulling me closer.

God! Her scent drives me wild. I jerk away, diving into her neck to taste her deliciousness. She moans.

My cock is a steel rod. Pain pulsing behind an ever-tightening zipper. It takes every ounce of self-control to keep from pushing against her.

I can't.

If we made love, skittish Melanie would be back in a heartbeat. She'd probably kick me out before the condom hit the trashcan and I'd be worse than square one. She'd never trust that I want anything more than one night with her body.

I've seen the love swirling in this town. Cartoon hearts bubble over happy couples everywhere I look. At least in my head.

Melanie wiggles against my front, but I tilt my hips away, hiding the evidence of my arousal with a groan. After a few torturous passes over those sweet lips, I dig for the willpower to pull away from temptation personified. Back to reality. Melanie's eyes are still closed, her breathing erratic as she clings to my biceps for dear life. The relaxation softening her face makes me feel ten-feet tall.

"Have dinner with me," I say, stroking the smooth line of those high cheekbones.

She blinks, momentarily stunned, and I smile, willing her not to pretend that kiss didn't make her want more.

Her throat works as she sucks those kiss-ravaged lips between her teeth. Stormy eyes land on my chest, tension filling the air as she debates her answer. My jaw clenches.

Finally, Melanie sucks in a deep breath, her gaze lifting to mine with a spark in those green depths. She smirks. "We can go to dinner, but my treat for all your help."

"What! No way." My scoff earns a squinty eye that rivals my mama's best glare, and I laugh. "Damn, woman." Holding her shoulders, I lean back, gaging her anger level. Smart men keep their women happy, but I'm not keen on our first date being her expense. "Look, how about I let you treat lunch this week... or breakfast?" I wink, just to distract Melanie from thinking too hard about arguing. "But dinner is mine."

Her bark of laughter releases the tight knot in my shoulders. "Little presumptuous with the breakfast, aren't ya?"

My eyebrows nearly hit my hairline and I clutch my chest as if wounded. "Never!" I scoff, adopting the British accent I'm so horrible at. "I'd never insult my lady in such a way. *Oomph—*" Melanie's hand slaps my stomach, but I count that full-grown grin as a complete win. "I only mean that for our first date, it's my treat."

She blinks. "First date?"

Instinctively, I cup the back of her head, tilting so she can't hide from my truth. "Melanie, I think you know I like you. I want you, yes. But I want to take you out, show you off. And by the look on your face, sooner rather than later, so you don't change your mind."

A soft lilt at the corner of her mouth gives me hope until her face falls and her eyes water. "Tyler, I... I just got out of relationship hell—"

Gently, I place a finger over her lips. "Shh... I get it. I just want to spend time with you." Her vulnerability tugs at my heart. I want to fix it.

Melanie cocks her head as she gazes up. "Why?"

I wink. "Why not?"

My joke relaxes her body, and she shakes her head, tipping forward to rest it on my chest. "You are too much."

I chuckle. "I've been told."

For a few minutes, we stand there, listening to each other breathe until my phone alarm vibrates, and I pull back. "Unfortunately, I need to get to Liza's this afternoon to finish a job, but if you're up for it, I'd love to pick you up later, showered and not in paint clothes. We can go someplace easy in town. No pressure. Just dinner."

That tentative smile gives me hope, even as she bites that thick lip I want to suck so badly and makes me wait. "Dinner." She lifts a threatening finger and pokes my chest. "Casual. And I get to pay you back another day."

I grin. "Second date. I'm not arguing."

"Shut up." She laughs, shoving me back toward the door. "Go. Get to work. I've got a big mess to clean up."

Guilt pauses my steps just before we get to the kitchen door. "I can stay and help."

She softens. "No. Go. Work. Do whatever you need to do. I've got this."

Sensing she needs space, I nod. "Okay. But I'll be back. Six o'clock."

Without waiting for confirmation, I lean over, stealing a kiss to hold me over through hours of work. Crouching under the dirty bug-covered crawl space at Liza's house won't be nearly as fun.

Maybe while I'm there, Liza will give me a few tips for convincing her gun-shy friend to take a chance on me.

Chapter Seven

Tyler

The bones in my wrist jar as my hammer swings, setting yet another nail in a piece of loose siding. I've already replaced the rotted boards on this side of the house, a process that took longer than expected, because of course it did.

Old farmhouses are notorious for random surprises during home repairs. This one is no exception.

The nest of squirrels who made their weather-protected home behind Liza's damaged wood did not enjoy my disruption. However, Smith has woken up with vermin inside their bedroom too many times. Apparently, the racoon yesterday was his last straw.

There's still a lot of work to do, but hopefully after this fix, Grandpa Hawke's old farmhouse will be airtight... finally.

Every weekend, I make progress, inside and out. Weekdays, I work at Dad's store and on my handyman business. There're always last-minute emergencies for the older residents of town.

Eventually, I want to grow into large scale remodels and renovations. That takes time and experience, though. It's a big reason I offered my help to Liza and Smith at near cost. After everything is done, their before and after photos will help upgrade my website for higher-end bookings.

The dumpster I left for Liza is half full now, but given the size of the yard, it shouldn't be a problem to take pictures with it out of the way. Liza cleared most of the junk downstairs before Smith and Fiona moved in for safety reasons, but she still has the whole upstairs to do. I'm sure more projects will pop up once we move her grandpa's trash to the bin outside.

I glance around at the spacious yard, visualizing Smith's daughter growing up here. I'll reinforce the tree swing when she's big enough, but there's room for a slide or treehouse. Depending on what she likes, she's got room to play ball or have tea parties by the big oak.

First, we need to finish. My goal is to have the front porch rebuilt by next weekend. Lumber is scheduled for Thursday. Smith helped me shore up the steps for safety, but redecking, sanding, and painting will make this place really shine. The photos are going to be freaking awesome!

Breathing new life into neglected properties is what I love.

Today, though, the monotony of squatting on the underside of Liza's porch is getting to me. My body is screaming, ready to quit. Could be my fixation on a certain dark-haired pixie. Wishing I could have stayed on her lips, instead of sweating my ass off out here.

"Busy morning?" Liza asks, popping up over my shoulder.

"Shit!" I drop my hammer, startled. "Jeezus, woman." I chuckle, hoping it hides that my brain was miles away in a tiny apartment over a beauty salon.

"Sorry." Liza has the decency to look chagrined, but it's not her fault I've lost my marbles.

"No worries. I just finished up." Smiling at Liza is easy. The sweet girl makes my friend so happy.

I stand, wiping my hands on the front of my pants so I can clean up. Liza checks out the repair while I organize my tools inside the toolbox.

"It looks great!" she says. "Thank you so much for finishing before the rain hit. We owe you so much." Liza wraps my neck in a hug, despite my sweaty state.

"Nah..." I grin at my childhood friend. "You guys are helping me out, too."

She shakes her head and laughs. "Not equally, though. Smith threatened that if he wakes up with another racoon in our bedroom, he's going to cook it for dinner." The twist of Liza's face tells me her thoughts on roadkill barbeque, but her impression of Smith has me cracking up.

"Don't worry." I pat the side of the freshly secured house. "You're locked tight now."

In a few months, spring will bloom with fresh foliage across the meadow, giving the farmhouse a new life. I'll be here for it. Hopefully, with a mutual friend on my arm to share the hot summer nights.

Speaking of, I glance at my watch, breathing a sigh that there's enough time to drop Dad dinner after I shower and still have time to grab a surprise for Mel.

Liza helps me carry my supplies to the truck despite my protest. It saves time, and I can't argue with that. "I'll see you guys tomorrow to seal the little vermin holes inside," I say, climbing into the cab.

"You wanna come by for dinner tonight?"

"Is Smith cooking racoon?"

"*Hah!* No. We're celebrating our meeting with the lawyer yesterday." The elation on Liza's face warms my heart and eases some of the tension I've felt for my best friend since his crazy ex dropped a surprise baby in his lap.

I hop out of the truck and wrap Liza in a hug. "So good news, then?"

Paranoia has eaten at all of us for the last month. Everyone is afraid that Fiona's drug addicted mother could pop back into her life and take her away. Smith is terrified he's not good enough, and nothing Liza nor I say gets through his thick skull. He deserves that little girl. And she's lucky to have him. No one will ever protect Fiona better than her dad. I know that.

When Liza pulls back, her eyes sparkle with tears, but she blinks them back, sniffling with a relieved smile. "Good news, definitely. We've got so much to talk about." She shifts from foot to foot, looking nervous, but that radiant smile eases the knot of worry in my stomach. "Smith took the weekend off to work on Tucker's catering plans. Next weekend, he's slammed."

"I've got plans tonight. But I can do dinner tomorrow if you guys are free."

"Sounds good. I'll let Smith know." Liza scans down my paint splattered T-shirt with a secretive smirk. "Hot date?"

A wash of heat warms my ears, but I nod. "I have a date. Yes." I climb up in the truck, cutting off further questions. "What can I bring tomorrow?"

She chuckles, but let's me get away with the secrecy... for now. "You know Smith, don't worry about bringing anything except your appetite. Now go shower. I don't want to make you late."

Nodding, I take one last look over Liza's shoulder at the home she and Smith are building together, and wave. A thrill washes away the pit of jealousy as I turn out onto the road, heading home to wash the stink off me. Maybe one day, Melanie wouldn't mind sharing my little fixer upper, as well. We could build it into a home, instead of just a place I rest my head.

Chapter Eight

Melanie

Gah! Why did I agree to this?

I toss my fifth outfit on the bed and backtrack to the box of clothes I retrieved this afternoon.

If I hadn't donated most of my clothes before I packed up, I might have something presentable to wear. Something in between worn-out leggings and the yuppy country club sweaters Aaron's mom bought me.

"Ugh! Those things can go to hell."

Digging a little deeper, I pull at the swatch of tangerine fabric sticking up from under a stack of clothes that fell from their hangers. What did I expect from boxes who have moved three times? I'm lucky they're intact and not chewed by mice or bugs, or whatever else lives in the back of garages.

I lay my favorite shirt across the bed to find the iron. That's a hell of a lot of wrinkles. If I think about that, though, I'll never stop sweating. The line of wetness at my hairline is already hard enough to get rid of. Tilting my head back, I search for the breeze of the ceiling fan, needing some relief. This thick mess is impossible to dry while rushing around.

"Argh!"

My phone blares the Lady A ringtone I set for Liza and I jump, setting the mini ironing board on my bed I had hidden in my closet. "Hey, girl!" I answer, slightly out of breath.

"Hey! Were you running?"

I spread my shirt out, laughing. "Nah, the last time I ran, it was for the last donut in the breakroom."

"Spsh... liar. You may be a newbie, but I know you better than that after hanging out with you that first night."

We share a chuckle, but it's hard to concentrate on what Liza's saying when the clock on my nightstand screams to move fast. I crank the iron to a delicate temperature and rush for the bathroom.

"Whatcha need, girlie?" I wet a cool rag and wipe the moisture from my neckline. Powder will help some, but I wanted to do more than the bare minimum make up I know how to apply.

"Smith and I want to invite you to dinner tomorrow night. We're having a few people over. The dining room is presentable, finally, and we want to celebrate."

"Nice! That's awesome!" I contemplate for a moment if Tyler will be at dinner as my hands work rollers into my hair. Chances are high. Tonight better go well, otherwise dinner is going to be awkward as hell tomorrow. "Can I bring anything?"

"Nah, don't worry about bringing anything. You're still unpacking."

I glance around the freshly scrubbed bathroom and laugh. Her fiancé was not the neatest person to clean up after. I might have to tease Smith a little bit. The least he could do is reward me with those fancy cooking skills.

"I'll be there. What time you want me?"

"Head over around six. We'll have a drink while Smith finishes up on the grill."

My stomach twists to hear so much love in my friend's voice. She sounds truly content. I never felt that with Aaron, so it's nice to see it's out there. But I'm not dwelling today. Those emotions do nothing but sink my self-esteem.

The flash of Tyler's warm brown eyes heating right before he kissed me is an easy distraction.

Digging through my makeup bag, I find the stick blush that I use because I can't manage the real thing without looking hookerish. Liza is updating me on the plans for tomorrow, so I hit the speaker button and prop my cell against the mirror to finish applying mascara.

"You there?"

Shit! I zoned out, trying not to make myself look like a spider.

"Sorry. Sorry. I was uh—what did you say?"

She laughs. "What's got you in the clouds?"

Heat rushes up my neck, adding better color to my face than I did. The problem is, I don't want to share my plans for tonight. Not yet.

Having a wedding canceled so close to the ceremony, and in such a mortifying way, is hard to stomach. It's a small town. If tonight is a bust, I couldn't take being the center of attention for the gossip mill again.

"Sorry. I'm rushing for an appointment. Can we just chat tomorrow when I get there?" Liza pauses, and I wonder if she's going to call me on my lie.

"No problem. I've got a great cranberry cocktail recipe I never got to try at Christmas. We'll turn it up and make the boys wait on us." That all but confirms Tyler's presence at dinner.

"Sounds good. I'll see you tomorrow."

"Awesome! Don't work too hard tonight," she says, the lilt in her voice sending my mind into the gutter.

We say our goodbyes with ten minutes to spare for ironing my shirt and getting ready. As I press the warm iron to what I hope is still my lucky shirt, a text chimes. Ugh! I don't have time for anything else. Tyler doesn't have my number yet, so I know he's not texting to cancel.

After a few passes, all the wrinkles are gone and I pull my shirt over my head, sighing as the fabric falls loosely over my soft tummy. I turn to the mirror and wiggle back and forth. It looks as good as I remember, forgiving and silky to the touch. Orange looks great with my skin and hair, even in the winter. The dipping neckline feels feminine and pretty, while the flowy sleeves cinch at the wrist to keep warm. It's confidence building. Exactly what I need going into a date with the hottest man on this side of the Mason-Dixon. Probably the other side, too.

I rummage through my small dresser, still sitting off the wall from our morning paint session and lift my favorite dark wash jeans from the bottom drawer. They hug my hips like Tyler's gaze does, at least when he thinks I'm not looking. He must like them.

Sitting on the bed, I jerk them over my socked feet just as Tyler's playful knock taps at the door. Jumping up, I grab my phone and run my fingers through the waves I curled my frizz into. The name on the screen drops my stomach.

Aaron: Call me. We need to talk.

The hell we do.

That text can sit right there until I get home.

Anger heats my blood, ratcheting my heart rate until it's thumping in my ears. Damn him. I was getting excited about this date without his dumbass popping in my head. After not hearing from him since the night I called off our wedding, I figured that was it. Thought he'd slunk away somewhere with the tramp he was buried in that night.

Immediately, I kick myself for calling names. She seemed as clueless as I was with that idiot.

Another knock sounds. Not demanding, but firm.

With older apartments, there's no doorbell to hear in the back-rooms. The thought of Tyler canceling popped into my head for a minute this afternoon, but he's here.

I breathe a sigh of relief. This distraction is exactly what I need after that text.

Determination spikes as I slam my phone on top of the dresser and leave it. "Coming," I call, hurrying for the door, feeling optimistic for the first time in ages.

Chapter Nine

Melanie

Before reaching for the handle, I suck in a deep breath and pat my hairline, hoping it hides how overheated I am.

When I open the door, Tyler is there, hotter than ever. A giant grin lights his face as he takes me in and I do the same. Sharp black jeans hug his strong thighs, leading to a sexy pair of brown boots that match his belt. A deep blue button down stretches across those muscular shoulders, cupping his chest and tapering to tuck into his narrow waistband with a pop of color that somehow heightens the sexiness of that tanned skin.

Cool air whips past me, offering a little relief as we both stand there staring at each other.

He's just more style than I expected from a small town handyman, and it's overwhelming. The moment the thought is in my head, guilt hits right behind it. Tyler doesn't deserve to be judged by stereotypes. Especially when they're usually wrong. The last person I picked looked good on paper and left a sour taste in my mouth.

"Hi," he says, tilting forward a bouquet of brightly colored wildflowers.

"Hey." I fight to keep my smile cool as I take the flowers. "Come on in. I'll put these in water."

One sweet gesture and I'm an overly excited pup. He shuts the door and follows me to the kitchen, where I grab one of the few vases I've unpacked and fill it with water. I glance at the man candy waiting for me and make a resolution. After these last few months of hellish stress, I'm going to enjoy tonight. Come hell or high water.

No thinking too hard.

No worrying about where this is going or not. I'm going to enjoy the fun for what it is and forget everything else.

"You look beautiful," Tyler says, his voice husky.

Okay, there may be a few other activities I could enjoy for one night as well.

"Thanks." I hide the heat in my face by focusing on the water-line. "You look very handsome yourself."

The tips of my ears burn, but I risk a glance at Tyler and find him beaming, chest puffed as his eyes scan my length. My nipples pebble inside the lace bra I wore for tonight and I shift my feet, trying desperately to hide my body's response to his blatant interest.

Aaron never looked at me like that. Not once. It's probably why he went exploring elsewhere. And right now, I'm stupidly happy he did.

"Am I dressed okay for dinner?" I set the vase in the center of my corner table and fold my hands in front of me, wishing he would take the choice out of my hands and whisk me back to the bedroom.

"You're perfect for dinner." Tyler strides to where my fluffy suede jacket hangs on a hook by the door and holds it out for me.

I blink. Okay, first date, best behaviors. Laying on the charm by helping date with her jacket. He waits for me to step forward and slide my arms in, brushing my hair out of the way as he sets the coat right. Did he just sniff my shampoo?

Glancing over my shoulder, I catch his chagrined smile and soften at the dusky rose coloring his cheeks. "Blueberries and lemon?"

He's too freaking cute. I nod, shoving down the self-doubt over someone paying such close attention. "It's my shampoo. The citrus wakes me up in the morning and makes me think of warm blueberry pancakes in bed."

Oh. My. God! Why did I say that out loud?

Tyler just smiles. "Me too." Lust flashes hot and fast in his eyes, but he steps back quick, easing some of the tension stealing my breath. "We'll have to make that happen one day."

"Ready?" He holds out his hand and I pause, wondering how I'm going to make it through the night when I'm waffling on a teeter totter of pent-up hormones.

"Let's go." I grab my clutch—and his hand—and follow that sexy backside out the door.

At his truck, Tyler opens my door, waiting until I buckle before he jogs around to climb in. I cross my hands in my lap, enjoying the leather, woodsy scent in the air. I can't tell if it's an air freshener, or just Tyler, but I wouldn't mind rolling around in it for a few hours either.

"So, where are we going?" I ask as Tyler pulls away from the curb. The streetlights highlight his afternoon stubble, bouncing off the freshly shined dashboard in a steady rhythm. The cab was clean last time I rode in it, but tonight it gleams, as if he detailed it special for our date. It's flattering.

His eyes dart my way. "You like Italian?" A nervous smile settles over his face as he focuses on the road.

"Love it."

The waning light gives me a front-row seat to his flitting emotions, but I don't want nerves on this date. I want him to relax, to make him feel as excited as he makes me.

Tyler's shoulders relax at my answer. "Awesome! I thought we'd get outside of town. Show you my favorite mom and pop, about halfway to the springs. It's called Gallo House. Have you heard of it?"

"Perfect. I haven't explored outside of Main Street since I moved to town."

I don't point out why. Instead, I focus on the countryside passing us by. Fields of cut wheat and dry grass spread for miles. Rows and rows of pines tower above, breaking occasionally for rolling farmlands and cottages. Wispy clouds streak the sky gray, hinting at snow. I hate snow. And the cold.

This has been the most depressing winter of my life.

A chill works down my spine, despite the heater blowing on high. Tyler covers my hand with his warmth, drawing me back to the present.

"Where did ya go on me?" He pulls our hands onto the center console and twines our fingers together as if it's the most normal thing in the world.

I study his furrowed brows, swallowing past the lump in my throat. "I'm good." Too much dwelling on negative lately. And Tyler really is sweet. It feels natural sitting beside him, like I don't have to put on a show or entertain.

Tyler's quiet, eyeing me from the side, but thankfully, he leaves it alone and changes the subject. "Wanna play twenty questions?"

A laugh bubbles up that surprises me, considering my train of thought. "Are we twelve?"

His grin is impossible. "People have accused me of worse," he says, squeezing my hand. "What's your favorite color?"

I squint my eyes, debating on giving him a hard time. Instead, I hold out my shirt and lift a brow.

"Orange?"

"Ding. Ding. Ding." Tyler beams, relaxing the last bit of knots tying up my stomach. "My turn. What was the craziest thing you got in trouble for as a kid?"

"Damn, woman! Going for the juggler." His rumbling laughter fills the cab as he slaps his chest playfully. Immediately, I hate the loss of his hand, but I hide it by tucking it into my lap. Tyler instantly pulls it back to center as if I stole his toy. "I get it. Gotta get ammo early." He sighs, pretending to be put out. "When Smith and I were eleven, we told our parents we were sleeping at each other's house."

"You weren't."

"Of course not. We went into the woods. You know us... big,bad, tough guys.Someone at school told us Big Foot stories, and we were convinced he lived in Kissing Springs. We checked out books, packed camp supplies, and staked out all night."

I crack up at the adorable image of a tiny Tyler and Smith's grumpy sourpuss in a child's body, going into the woods in search of an urban legend.

"Did you find anything?" I ask, masking my snort inside a cough. Tyler hears and smirks. Damn him.

"We found out that two young boys don't know enough to check the weather before packing a bookbag full of snacks and some sleeping bags."

"Yikes! What happened?"

"A downpour hit two hours into our search. We hid under a giant oak, pretending the lightning and thunder didn't scare us." Tyler gets this faraway look, lost in the memories. "Turns out, Spring Creek floods in the rain. Who knew?" His self-deprecating smirk is reminiscent of a naughty little boy who got caught. It's adorable and draws me into the story even more. "We were soaked, trapped, and snuggled together, shivering. Two fools who should have known better."

"Aww, you were kids."

"Yeah, but it wasn't our first time camping. We knew better than to travel that far." He shakes his head. "Our bags were full of candy bars and Gatorade and disposable cameras we stole from Dad's store.Not exactly boy scout material."

"You stole!" I gasp, feigning shock.

"Didn't think you were out with a bad-boy, huh?"

I smack his arm, glowering at the sting of hitting that rock-hard bicep. "Hardly bad boy." I shake out my fingers. "I could take ya."

The corner of Tyler's lips twitch, fighting a smile. I don't exactly scream badass ninja woman.

"No doubt." He nods with mock seriousness. "If you couldn't, I'd happily teach you happily."

My mind hits the gutter for what else he could teach me. I clear my throat. "So, uh... what happened?"

Tyler glances at me from the corner of his eye before turning his attention back to the road.

"Well, after hours in the rain, we got the bright idea to cross the creek, and I almost lost Smith to the current. Thankfully, he grabbed a limb and pulled himself to shore, but it freaked me the hell out. We ditched our bags and started running through the woods."

"You poor things."

He chuckles. "Yeah. Turned out, our dads got wind of our stupidity and had search parties out hunting, too. Uncle Tucker found us halfway home and radioed my dad and the police chief. We had to apologize to the group of volunteers, the fire department... everyone. It was mortifying. Thankfully, Dad was so relieved he didn't exactly punish me. Just watched me reeeally close for a few months." He drags out the word and I get the gist his dad held the reins a little tighter than he lets on.

By the time Tyler's done with his story, he's pulling into a parking lot beside a large cinderblock building painted with the Italian countryside. Scenes of grape plants rolling over vineyards litter the side of the building, creating a beautiful mural that Tyler parks in front of.

"It's beautiful." One of my dreams is to visit every tourist trap on that wall, from the vineyards to the iconic cities, coastal roadways to the monuments and art.

Tyler follows my gaze, his expression softening. "It is. Their daughter painted that. She's an artist but has a hard time turning her passion into... more. Right now, she's applying to art schools everywhere she can."

"She's good," I offer, sensing how much his big heart feels for this family.

"She is."A brilliant smile lights up his face before Tyler hops out of the truck and jogs around to open my door.

"I could get that."

"You could, but I can too."

Hopping down, I take his offered arm, shaking my head. "You are too much."

Tyler chuckles. "Never said I wasn't."

As we enter the restaurant, it's like we're transported into another world. Art déco paintings cover the walls. Two massive candle candelabras split the room, hanging from rustic chains that accent the dark wood everywhere. Mustard colored texture streaks the Tuscanwalls, espresso glaze darkening the crevices.

"Tyler!" A squat woman in linen pants and a black ruffled top rushes up and wraps her arms around my startled date. "So lovely to have you in, my boy. Who's this?" She peaks around Tyler's massive shoulder with that sweet, grandmotherly smile. "I'm Mrs. G, sweetheart."

He slides to the side, pulling my hand to bring me into the conversation. "This is my date, Melanie."

"Ahh, beautiful name for a beautiful lady." She leans in, kissing both of my cheeks and catching me off guard.

"Umm, thank you. You have a lovely place here."

"Oh, it does its job." She waves off my compliment and gazes up at Tyler, pride obvious in her smile. "We wouldn't be where we are without this man here, though."

His cheeks redden adorably. "How are things going, Mrs. Gallo?"

She pats his arm as she takes his elbow, dragging him, and by extension, me, to a red vinyl booth in the back corner of the restaurant. "Things are wonderful, thanks to you. Vince cooks up a storm on that new grill. He has a new mushroom fontina, I'll bring you." She kisses her fingertips and sends them into the air with a smack. "Bellissimo."

Before we can even respond, she drops the two menus in her hand and hurries off to the kitchen. "Wow." Tyler lifts a brow expectantly, waiting. "She loooves you." He snorts at my sing-song voice, but the brightest smile lights up his face that warms me inside.

"She's a sweet woman." I reach for the menu and flip open the heavy leather cover while Tyler scans the wine list. "Would you like a bottle of wine?"

"I could do a glass of Chianti."

I duck my eyes, feeling the awkwardness of a first date returning. That battle of not ordering anything too expensive since he's paying.

While we wait, I peruse the pasta dishes, something else I never allow myself on a date. They look amazing! But... I slide over to the leaner dishes.

Damn common sense.

Damn carbs that go straight to my hips.

Tyler watches me, increasing my discomfort. "The chicken on a brick sounds fabulous."

"Chicken?" A deep V forms between his brows .

"It looks good," I say defensively.

He chuckles. "As long as that's it and you're not trying to eat like a bird in some misguided date protocol."

I bite my tongue between my molars. He needs to stop with those idealistic, 'you can be yourself' lies.

He's saved by an older gentleman in a black polo who sets a wooden plank on the table between us. The restaurant name emblazoned on his breast matches the apron hanging from his hips. Three perfectly charred bruschetta with sliced mushrooms, crumbles of cheese, and some sort of rich drizzle, making my mouth water.

I moan. "These smells delicious." I lean in for a better whiff.

The chef grins, his chin lifting with pride as he takes my hand and brings the knuckles in for a kiss. "Grazie, bella. Il cibo qui è amore."

Tyler's smirk says I'm the only clueless person at the table. "Watch it, Vince. Keep your charm in the kitchen where it belongs."

He chuckles, slapping Tyler on his massive shoulder before leaning in for a familial hug. "No worries, son. I'm just showing you how to woo your tesoro."

I hide a laugh behind my hand, watching Tyler's ears turn red. "Don't scare her away, old man."

"Nonsense, my boy." He turns to me. "This is a good one, you know. Protect his heart."

Tyler groans, dropping his head in his hands, but the sweet older man grabs his head and pulls it into his big belly with a chuckle.

"Get out of here, old man." Tyler playfully swats his hands off his head, coming out of the hug disheveled and beet red. His wavy hair curls out over his ear, sticking up at odd angles on the back of his head.

It's flipping adorable.

The chef takes a step back, laughing,and gives Tyler one last knock on the shoulder. "I'll send Kat out for your order." With one more wink in my direction, he turns on his heels with way more grace than the squat little man should have. "Kat! Ka-at! Tavolo!"

"Holy crap. That was a lot," I say as Tyler straightens his hair, his eyes warm and relaxed, watching the chef disappear through the swinging door.

"He is." There's not an ounce of venom in Tyler's voice. No butt-hurt expression over his messy hair or from being manhandled by a little old man.

I don't mean to compare so much, but it taunts at me how different the man in front of me is than my ex, and every part of me sings for it.

We only get a breath before Mrs. Gallo is back to take our drink order. Tyler orders my wine and a Peroni for himself and then she's gone with a secretive smile.

"How long have you known them?"

Tyler's shoulders stiffen. His eyes darkening into endless pools as he looks away. I feel the weight of his next words. "Mrs. G collects people, draws them into her orbit." Warmth fills his gaze when it settles on the sturdy woman, pouring two waters and twisting a cap from a bottle of wine behind the bar. "And well, I came here a lot after my discharge. It's on the way to my favorite spot."

"Spot? Like fishing spot? Hiking spot?" Those soulful eyes burn into my secrets.

"Thinking spot. Just so happens it's at the tail end of the longest trail in the Springs. Let me wear my brain out and work my body to exhaustion. The Gallo's fed me and kept my thoughts from going into dark places for many months after I got home." Pain flits over that gorgeous face, making my palm itch to reach out, to comfort. He shakes his head. "There's this gorgeous pool of hot springs at the end. Soaking away your feelings is almost as good as eating them." His self-deprecating chuckle eases the tension that settled over the table like a wet blanket.

"But you'd have to hike all the way back soaked. Didn't that... chafe?"

"Who said I swam in my clothes?" My mouth drops at the naughty smirk staring back at me. "What? Think I'm too dull for a little skinny dipping?"

I swallow. "No... I just..." I'm having a hard time not picturing it and I *will not* admit that out loud. Instead, I go for another hard to admit truth. "I've never swam—without clothes."

"Hmm... may have to rectify that one day."

And... I have officially swallowed my tongue.

"Here you go." Mrs. Gallo saves my burrowing under the table with the arrival of our drinks. I take a fortifying sip, surprised by how smoothly the house wine goes down. "How about dinner? Y'all know what you want?"

Tyler waves to me, ever the gentleman, letting me go first. He doesn't do that asshole cave man thing of ordering for me. Smart man. Smiling, I order my craved chicken and laugh when Tyler clutches his chest and shakes his head.

"The usual," he says before narrowing his eyes at me. "After, we'd love a slice of your tiramisu, Mrs. G. Gotta make sure my lady is full."

A growl slips out at that self-satisfied smirk and both of them jerk in surprise. Mrs. Gallo fighting and failing to hide her grin.

"Did you just growl at me?"

To say my face feels like a volcano is an understatement. Huge, supreme understatement!

Instead of admitting the truth, I shrug, feigning innocence while Mrs. Gallo chuckles her way back to the kitchen to put in our order.

Chapter Ten

Tyler

S exy as hell.

That's what she is.

Every little blush makes me wonder how far the rouge goes under that blouse.

It's been impossible to keep my mind out of the gutter, especially after admitting she's never been skinny dipping.

God, if I were younger—and stupider—I'd try to end the night with a little dare to jump.

Then, that ball-busting growl... *Fuck!*

Under the table, I adjust my out-of-control cock, praying she doesn't notice with the tablecloth overhang. Mrs. Gallo would knock my head if she saw. I need a distraction from the wildfire sitting across from me.

"So, not part of our twenty questions, but how did you and Liza meet?" Damn, there goes those rosy cheeks again.

"We um... she helped organize my bridal shower, which turned out to be more of a bachelorette party?"

I cock my head at the lilt in her voice. "Did you not know going in?" Melanie's forehead hits her palms, hiding her laughter. I tug them down, holding both hands under mine on the table, just to lean down for a peek under those dropped lashes. "What is it?"

She sneaks a peek toward the empty restaurant. "You know Liza's friend Lennox?"

"Yeah, we went to high school together."

"Oh. Well, uh, she planned the party at the strip club in town."

"The male revue?" I chuckle, because most of the women in town fawn all over Dillon and his dancers. They definitely don't whisper their names like a dirty little secret. Even though the men strip to a variety of boxer or thongs, few call them strippers. "Did you have fun?"

"Sure, but it was not how I expected to spend the night." Melanie giggles. "She threw crazy penis decorations all over the table. Balloons. Cupcakes. All with colorful... male parts, some crooked, big, small... It was crazy. And Liza and I were embarrassed as hell."

"I thought girls loved screaming over half-naked men."

"Sure..."

By the time she's done describing the craziest, acrobatic routine by a guy I know to be a new hire, her face is the color of her wine and I'm cracking up.

My beer is gone—faster than planned—but conversation with Melanie is just so damn easy. So easy, I don't notice when the teenage runner brings out our plates until Melanie hums her pleasure over her glazed chicken. God! She needs to stop doing that.

"How's everything taste?"

I start, too focused on Melanie's lips biting around her fork to notice Mrs. G walking up to my left. My unit commander would kick my ass, but I suck in a deep breath, not feeling that quick panic of the old days.

Being the sweet woman she is, Katrina rubs my back apologetically. "Sorry, Ty."

"No worries." I glance down, staring at my favorite manicotti, instead of her concern. "Dinner is delicious."

"Yes, ma'am. Everything is wonderful," Melanie says, gushing.

Mrs. G leans in to refill our water glasses as a giant clap of thunder rattles above us. She jumps. "Dio Mio! Would you two like another round?"

"Sure. Might as well if it's going to rain on us." Melanie sips her nearly finished wine and, for the first time since we met, seem carefree and relaxed.

"I'm good for now." I shrug. "Wet driving, not fun."

Mrs. Gallo pats my shoulder. "You're a good boy, Tyler. I'll be back in a few."

When she's gone, Melanie leans in. "We can leave early if you want. Beat the storm."

I stare at those catlike irises and find no judgement. No disappointment. Just open honesty. Still, I hesitate. "After the work it took to convince you to go to dinner with me?"

She chuckles and forks a slice of asparagus, chewing it thoughtfully as she takes me in. "We can get dessert to-go and grab coffees on the way back to my place." My eyebrows hit my hairline. They must. But Melanie swats my hand. "For. Dessert."

"I am craving something sweet." *And nothing we can order on a menu.*

"Ugh. Come on." She smirks. "I'm going to tell Mrs. Gallo on you."

"*Hah!*" My hands fly to the air as I lean back in the seat. "I don't know what you're talking about. I'm an innocent boy who helped save their kitchen after a grease fire."

"Ooh, sneaky." That glare would kill if not for that tiny hint of a smile.

To rub it in a little more, I give her my best dimpled grin. The one that wins cheek pinches from the old biddy club.

Mrs. Gallo picks that moment to walk up with Melanie's wine, so I don't get to push her buttons anymore. Melanie narrows her eyes at me briefly, but then aims a sweet, charming smile at our proprietor. "Thank you so much, Mrs. Gallo. We decided to take dessert to go, if you don't mind boxing it up for us."

Her responding wink is downright salacious and Melanie's mouth drops. "I got you. I got you. Two shakes of a lamb's tail and you kids can get out and enjoy your evening."

Once she's gone, Melanie leans in. "I'm not used to this." Her gaze follows Katrina's receding back.

"What? Nosy old women?"

She shrugs. "I guess, just... everybody knowing everything I do."

"Small towns."

Melanie is quiet as we check out, lost in her thoughts. We grab our to-go containers, hesitating when we reach the door. Outside, the sky has opened up and even without lightning, we're going to get drenched running to the truck.

"Here. Hold this." I pass Melanie our plastic baggie of food and slide off my jacket, angling it over her head to block the rain.

"Wha—you don't have to..."

Before she can argue, I use my body to wrap around and steer her out the door, taking the brunt of the deluge on my back. "Let's go." She squeals as we sprint for the cover of my truck. I jerk the door open, lifting her elbow to help her climb inside with our food balanced in her lap.

"You didn't lock your door?" she asks, her eyes wide.

"Small town."

I grin, leaning over our takeout to snap her buckle. Melanie's quick intake of breath pushes her plump breast against the orange fabric I'd love to peel off. Just not tonight. That would be a guaranteed label of one and done in her mind. Not having that.

However, resisting that plump pout stained red with her wine... impossible.

Her surprised squeak when I grasp the tip of her chin and hold her in place for a quick taste... delicious.

Nothing scandalous, though the soft give reminds me of how her body felt pressed against mine. Those luxurious curves test my control. I've always preferred a woman with more than a handful, with thighs thick enough to hold her up while I press her ass against a wall and sink myself into heaven.

With all my blood heading away from my brain, it's a Herculean effort to keep our kiss light.Brushing our lips. Keeping my tongue jailed for a semblance of control. When Melanie moans against my lips, her tongue flicking in a tease, I nearly explode.

Slowly, I pull back, smiling against her lips when she tries to follow. "We better get going before the Gallos come out here and toss a bucket of water on us."

She giggles, flipping my wet hair off my forehead. "You couldn't get any wetter."

"You could." My wink earns another laugh, a gold medal with this woman, but I back up when she swats my chest and close the door. It's fun to play with Melanie, to see her opening up, but I have to watch myself.

Inside the truck, I crank the heat and shake the water from my hair like a dog. Another squeal. "Oh, my god! What are you?"

"I'm your comic relief, baby."

Her laughter dies away as I pull out onto the mountain road. However, that heated gaze on the side of my face shifts the air in the cabin. "I've never met anyone like you."

I glance over. "Is that a good or bad thing?"

She leaves me suffering for a few impossible seconds. "It's a relief," she says, finally putting me out of my misery.

My chest swells, and I reach across the console, entwining our fingers in the center to focus on the road. With the rain and curves taking us back to town, I want to be as careful as possible. "You still good with coffee pit stop?"

"Sure."

We fall into a comfortable silence as we drive toward the place I frequent on the outskirts. The one away from all the small town eyes that make Melanie nervous. Rain patters the few cars in the parking lot. I assume the bare night employees, but at least it's not the downpour we left with.

When I help Melanie down from her seat, her wild curls have doubled in size, and I have a hard time not pointing that out. I don't think she'd find the humor. Wisely, I keep my mouth shut and my hand on the small of her back as I guide Melanie in front of me through the door.

Bells jingle overhead, alerting an employee in the back. "Welcome, y'all."

"Hey, Brit. Can I get my usual?"

"Sure thing." The young barista waits while Melanie scans the board.

"I'll have a café macchiato." She turns a brilliant smile to me. "It'll go great with our tiramisu." I can't help but beam at the brightness that's a hundred-eighty degrees from her lukewarm agreement to tonight's date.

"Ahem." A deep throat clearing behind us draws my attention.

Melanie's shoulders lock, her body turning to stone before she even turns to find the source. I slide closer automatically, sensing the change in the air. My fists clench, bracing for a fight when I see the owner of that voice.

"Look who we have here." I never met the woman, but there's no doubt the stiff-collared, plaid-skirted lady looking down her equine nose at us is Aaron's country club mother. The one who gave Melanie so much trouble. Ice-cold eyes lock on where my arm circles Melanie and she sneers. "I see you wasted no time."

Sharp eyes rake down my body, stripping me bare in the middle of the linoleum floor like a piece of prime rib she's evaluating for Christmas dinner. The heat there is wholly inappropriate for a woman her age.

Hell, I'd already be out that door if not for the urge to block Melanie from their viciousness. Instead, I move slightly in front of her and lock Aaron, who's attached to his mother's hip, in a stare down. His face sours when he notices my hand dropped protectively in the center of Melanie's back.

She's silent, tension vibrating the length of her spine. I expect a showdown, a bitch slap... something. Not for Melanie to completely ignore the two intruders into our pleasant evening to snatch her coffee.

"You're just going to ignore us after the embarrassment you caused."

Melanie jerks back as if slapped. My mouth falls open in shock, but Melanie, her eyes just brim with tears as she stares at the older woman.

It pisses me off, and my fist clinch, wishing I could smack this bitch of a woman. My girl doesn't deserve her vitriol.

"Exactly what embarrassment do you think she caused? From my view, it seems your son is the one who can't keep it in his pants."

"Spsh..." She waves a manicured hand in the air as if I'm being silly. "My boy made an indiscretion. It would have kept quiet if she knew how to handle her business. Maybe if she took care of herself, he wouldn't have strayed in the first place."

"Excuse me! How dare you blame her?"

"She embarrassed our family." The woman has the nerve to tip her head up in the air as if her son didn't hurt another human being with his actions. Rage rolls through me. A tidal wave blocking out all other thoughts than punching Aaron in his smug face.

"Does your mama always talk for you, prick? Does she wrap your dirty little dick for you, too?"

Aaron's face turns molten. "Mind your business, hick."

I step forward. "Or what?"

He pales, taking a tiny step behind his mother and Melanie shakes her head, placing a calming hand on my forearm. "Don't bother." She turns back to the counter. "Can you hurry, please?" she begs, her voice cracking.

It pulls my attention from the mama's boy in favor of blocking Melanie from their view. I reach into my back pocket and pull two twenties out just as the barista snaps on our lids. She hasn't rung us up yet, but I drop more than enough to cover our treats just to get us out of this situation faster. I don't like how quiet Melanie is, or how much her hands tremble against the countertop.

"I was going to pay for that," she says under her breath.

"It's okay, baby. I got you." I take my coffee from the shell-shocked teenager and force a smile that I hope doesn't scare the poor girl. We need to get out of here before I'm sued for assault. This dumbass wouldn't think twice, and I don't need that kind of stress in my life.

Without another word, I curl Melanie under my arm and aim for the door. "Enjoy your mama's teat, dumbass." Melanie snorts, and it feels like more of a victory than getting the last word on that loser.

Still, their interruption punched a hole in our date bubble, draining the easy atmosphere between us. Like ripping a Band-Aid off past baggage. Whether Melanie wanted me in her business or not, one chance meeting threw me into the deep end.

And I'm not mad at it.

Chapter Eleven

Melanie

My hand shakes as I slide my key in the door of my tiny studio. What the hell has become of my life?

Who did I piss off to earn this stellar luck? Seriously?

The lock sticks, adding insult to injury.

Tyler's warmth crowds my back. "Easy…" He reaches over my shoulder and jiggles the key. The door pops open easily, and I sigh. "Go on into the living room. I'll grab plates for dessert." That soothing drawl is a balm after running into Aaron, making it easy to follow directions with our to-go containers.

Privacy will give me time to breathe. Time to shake off the funk that man puts me in. Tyler's presence is a large, protective barrier against the world. Even as he disappears into the other room, I feel his safety, along with his eyes.

It's just… a lot.

After hanging my drenched coat over the back of a chair, I head for the not-so-comfy couch I need to replace. Another expense I won't get to until I build my business strong enough in this town.

That thought still swirls in my head a few minutes later when Tyler walks out. Two water bottles, forks, napkins, and a small square plate tuck against his chest. The spring leaves and yellow daisies decorating my kitchenware remind me of the bright, happy home I bought them for. The one I thought I'd build after the wedding. One or two kids running around sneaking cookie treats before dinner.

"You okay?" Tyler's deep baritone releases the pinch of stress in my chest, and I sigh.

"Yes. I'm fine."

"Uh, oh." The laughter in his voice draws me up short, my stack of supplies held tight against my chest. "You know what it means when a woman says she's fine?"

"Ugh…" I roll my eyes. "I saw that movie too, and I will tell you, we are not amused."

Tyler cocks a brow. "We?"

"Yes. The universal 'we'. Women. No one appreciates being told they are freaked out, insecure, neurotic, and emotional."

"Hey! Don't blame the messenger."

"Oh, shush!" I swat Tyler's chest, earning another laugh as he flops in the middle of the couch. His massive size shrinks the extra space as he slides in close, dropping his armload of supplies on my little coffee table.

Instead of diving into dessert, he sits back and pulls my hand into his lap. "Really, though, are you okay... after tonight?"

"You mean, after you got a crash course on the past two years of my life?"

"Those people are not your life." His venom surprises me, but I can't bear to look in his eyes. If I saw pity... "Look, I'm serious. You got rid of that cancer before he dragged you down."

My lips purse, and lean forward for a bottle of water, my throat drier that the Sahara. I'm tired of those people taking up space in my head. In fact, the more I think about the cocky smirk on Aaron's face as his mother berated me, the angrier I get. Anger fills the hole left behind after Aaron cheated. It's the life raft keeping me afloat among the whispers behind my back.

"They're out of my life now."

"Yeah, but anyone talking to you that way hurts. Especially someone like him... he doesn't have the right."

"No shit." Tyler's eyebrows raise. "Sorry. I'm just—I can't talk about him anymore. I can't believe how much I gave up for—for nothing."

"Not for nothing. I get he ain't worth the brain cells, but you're building a new life here." Tyler tucks a piece of loose hair behind my ear. "Give this town a chance. I promise, it'll be worth it."

My lips snap closed. How can someone be so optimistic? Aren't military men more cynical? Seen the worst in the world and all that...

Tyler lets his hand fall away. "Why don't we have dessert?"

I smile. "Sure."

Sitting back, I watch Tyler make himself a home, spreading our coffee-flavored treat onto the plate before leaning back into the couch cushions. "How about some T.V.? Unless you want to kick me out as fast as possible."

Laughing, I snatch his fork and take a bite of the coffee-flavored treat. "I have no idea how you can make me laugh right now. But no, I'm not in a hurry to push you out."

The corner of Tyler's lips twitch and I grab the remote, cursing when my *recently watched* list populates the big screen. All it takes is one quirked eyebrow for my face to heat.

"Shut up."

"Whaa… I said nothing."

"It's that face." I circle his dancing features with a finger, warning.

"What's wrong with my face?" he asks, his voice pitching hilariously. A quick hand snatches the remote, holding it to the side so I can't reach it without throwing myself into his chest. As tempting as that is.

"You were about to make fun of me." Tyler's grin spreads from ear to ear.

"Me? Noo…"

To pay him back for stealing the remote, though, I steal the tiramisu plate from his lap and take a bite. Curling my feet underneath me keeps me from leaning in closer as I hold his mock glare.

Squinting at Tyler, I drag a bite of rich, espresso-dusted mousse into my mouth. "I'm going to eat all of this. Just to punish you."

"Watching you eat it will make up for it." He eyes my lips like a chocolate topped sundae, sending a rush of heat to the tips of my ears that I blok.

Ignoring that minefield, I let the fork clink to the china and reach for my coffee instead. "Will you just pick something already?" My brain frazzles as I lean back against the couch arm. Distance for sanity. That's what I need.

Tyler has other ideas. He pulls my feet in his lap and slips off my wet shoes, locking my socked feet under his forearm as he sits back with his cup, my remote, and a smile.

"Which is your favorite?"

I cut my eyes, watching his expression as he scrolls through listings for *The Bachelor* and all its reality love partners. My collection of Ramsey creations, Top Chef, and Guy Fieri, gives him pause. Those sinfully full lips pursing before he continues scrolling. His thumb lazily rubs the inside of my ankle, calling for me to wiggle closer and pull away at the same time.

"We can put on a movie," I offer, hoping to end the insanity.

"Why? Your entire screen is a smorgasbord of reality T.V."

"You don't want to watch that."

"Why not? I like drama... as long as it's not mine. Or my friends. Gordon Ramsey screaming over raw scallops, forehead vein popping like my first drill sergeant at bootcamp."

"Aaron never watched these shows with me. He thought they were stupid."

"Aaron's stupid." I snigger at his matter-of-fact tone, and the third grader level comeback. Except there's nothing childish about that flash of anger darkening those soft brown eyes. The heat there strokes me, his gaze tracing the length of my jean covered legs like a lover's hand. "I'm pretty sure there are a lot of things Aaron didn't do for you."

"Got that right," I mumble, turning my attention to the T.V. "Put the latest season of the race show on. I'm only one episode in. I'll catch you up."

For the next hour, Tyler asks questions. Rags on bitchy characters and screaming couples. And cheers for the older—less likely to succeed—contestants. He's freaking adorable. At the end of the episode, he hits the next button, and we roll through two more, our coffees and treats long gone.

Unfortunately, the caffeine can't make up for the fact I've run on empty these past few weeks, and my head keeps falling to the back of the couch. Every now and again, I jerk upright and see the show still running. Tyler mirrors my motion, his head falling at an incredibly uncomfortable angle that no doubt would hurt tomorrow.

He's sprawled like a little boy. That flop of hair falling across his forehead adds to the man's cuteness, which should be impossible given his superhero level muscles and the constant five o'clock shadow I'd love to rub my fingers across.

Without thinking, I tug his shoulder, scooching to the side when Tyler snuggles into my stomach, mumbling in his sleep. His arm acts like a vise and in my sleepy state, I feel protected, treasured. And damned if my fingers don't dive into that floppy mop falling across his eyes just before I crash into sinful dreams.

The dream goes on forever. Me, blindly following broad shoulders through the woods toward the springs. The trail winding until a beautiful clearing opens with a trickling waterfall calling to me across a flat of wildflowers. I reach for the beauty, only to notice the sun isn't the only thing streaking through the canopy. I'm butt-ass naked.

The shoulders I followed like the Pied Piper turn, undressing on the sandy bank. A silver button snaps free from those baggy cargos, and as the zipper snicks lower, I feel myself floating. Floating away from the gorgeous water and even more gorgeous man, away from the dirty reveal making my mouth water in anticipation.

Chapter Twelve

Melanie

"Don't moan like that, Princess."

A sleepy rumble vibrates under my ear that sounds too much like a moan itself.

"Mmm…"

"Holy hell."

My weight shifts, drawing me away from the last fuzzy images of my dream. Fingers grip my thighs and squeeze, lifting me higher and I startle, latching my arms around the anchor holding me. "What's going on?"

"I'm carrying you to bed, sweetheart."

"What? Wait! Put me down." I wiggle in Tyler's grip, and he groans when my breasts accidentally rub against his chest. "Sorry… ugh, Tyler, I'm heavy. Put me down." His answering chuckle sends a flush up my neck that stops my wiggling. No need to add extra strain.

"What the hell are you talking about, woman?" As if to prove a point, he tosses me a few inches in his arms and catches me easily.

"Rude awakening much?"

"Just proving a point," he says, pushing through my bedroom door.

"Okay, fine, muscle man. Put my fat ass on the bed."

He stops, his arms locking around the thick thighs I hate with a passion. "You need to watch how you talk about yourself."

I kick. "Come on, just put me down."

"No."

"What do you mean, no?"

Tyler's eyes flash, but the stupid, immovable tree stays planted. "Take it back."

"Take what back?" I kick again, wiggling my butt to get free. Surprise... his grip tightens, and despite the ferocity darkening his normally friendly gaze, I don't feel danger from the big oaf. His irritation reminds me of a bulldog protecting his owner.

"You're beautiful," he says, resting my rear end on the mattress. His masculine smell clings to my skin, even after he straightens. Thick forearms cross over his chest, adding to the stubborn set of his jaw. "I knew those assholes got to you tonight. But are you really going to let them win?"

Fucking arrogant prick!

Pissed, I scramble to my knees on the bed, getting eye to eye with the overbearing jackass. I shove at his chest. "I'm not letting them win, dammit. You have no idea—"

Tyler rushes forward, cutting off the tirade in my head over all the BS that Aaron and his mom put me through these last few weeks. Rough hands dive into my hair, holding my head still as his lips crash down. I gasp and Tyler takes full advantage, diving in. His tongue slides smoothly along mine before drawing out and bringing me with him. My hands fall to his shoulders instinctively, fingernails digging in, both in irritation and holding on for dear life.

The kiss isn't slow and timid like this morning.

There's no testing or asking for permission.

Every ounce of annoyance pours into the press of our lips. Our bodies melt into each other as our teeth clash, causing Tyler to soften his grip on my face.

"Sorry." His voice is hoarse, sending a rush of wetness down below as his thumb trails along my jaw. "I planned to be a gentleman and carry you to bed after we fell asleep. But I can't listen to you talk about yourself that way."

My heart squeezes. "I'm fine, Tyler." I tug his hands free, needing some space from the intensity. "You're sweet, but my feelings are not your problem. We're friends. Or friends of friends. I don't know."

Tyler's face falls, but he lifts to full height, giving me a couple of inches to breathe. His jaw ticks and it's one of the sexiest things I've ever seen. "We're more than that and you know it."

I shake my head and look away. Darkness shrouds my bedroom, which is probably why I can be this honest. That, and Tyler is out of my league enough to settle expectations. He's a sweet man. But no use putting on a fake façade for someone to like you when there's no point.

"Look, I did let myself go. Apparently, I ate my feelings when dealing with Aaron." I laugh, but there's no humor in this situation. Shaking my head, I push Tyler's hulking frame back so I can step off the bed. Now that I'm fully awake, I need to brush my teeth and get ready for sleep. Not continue this ridiculous standoff. "I don't care right now. My emotions are on hiatus for a while."

"Shame. And that's your choice. Although I reserve the right to prove you wrong."

I sigh when he doesn't budge. His face is as immovable as his mammoth body.

He leans down, lining our bodies up, chest against much firmer chest, soft middle to what no doubt hides a six-pack. "We will take our time, Melanie. But I want you to know… you are fucking hot." His arm bands around my middle, lifting. "Your curves. They drive me up a goddamn wall. Can't you tell?"

At this cheated height, a prominent bulge fitting perfectly into the crease at my thighs. The friction triggers a yearning that's hard to ignore. Especially when his wide palm spreads across my lower back, pressing me close.

I've held myself in check every single time I see you, woman. I want more than a quick romp. I only haven't tossed you on this bed, because I want to give you time." Tyler bends, trailing his lips up my jawline to my ear. "Now, hearing you talk about yourself that way, pissing me off. I need a woman who can handle me. Crave it." The pulse of his hips leaves no doubt about what he needs handled. "Boney waifs do nothing for me. I want an ass to grab, breasts to smother myself in." He nips at the tip of my earlobe, causing a whine to slip past my lips as I wiggle, this time not for freedom.

If only I could beg Tyler to toss me on the bed and prove his words.

Instead of begging, I tug his thick mop of hair away from my sensitive neck. His eyes flare. "You're insane," I rasp, tilting my hips away, needing relief from the fabulous friction.

His grin lights up the darkness. "Never said I wasn't." I roll my eyes, but stop when a callused palm cups my face, tipping my head back for his piercing gaze. "I wanted to be a gentleman tonight."

"Gentleman are overrated." I swallow the lump of fear trapped in my throat and stroke down Tyler's rippling chest. "I've had the passionless gentleman. He turned out to be a toad."

"Fuck that!" Tyler tosses my weight back onto the bed like I'm a sack of dog food.

I squeal, laughter bubbling up from the ridiculousness of the romantic fantasy acting itself out in my bedroom.

"Assholes who can't take care of their women aren't gentle-men." Tyler's voice is gravel as he crawls toward me, biceps bulging. A solid foot separates our bodies as he bends down, rubbing his nose along mine. "Do you want me to leave?"

"What?" He's asking that after setting every nerve on edge.

"I told you what I want. If you need time, tell me to go now."

My smile fades, my brain stumbling over what he's asking. "Tyler, I can't make decisions tonight." But I don't want this feeling to stop. I can't say that out loud.

"I understand." His smile softens as gravity brings his hip to my side, lining his warmth along my body like a blanket. Tyler kisses my forehead and I groan, refusing to be slotted into that unsexy friend-zone. Even if that's where we should stay.

"I don't think you do." Deciding to be selfish for once in my freaking life, I tug his body close. "I don't want you to go. "How often does a girl have a muscled god in her bed?

A bravery takes over I've never felt before and I reach up, running the tips of my fingers under the hem of Tyler's loosened shirt. Blood pounds through my ears, as hot as the molten eyes pinning me to the bed. Tyler waits, letting me stroke his warm skin, that narrow dusting of hair that disappears under his belt. His sharp intake of breath spurs me on, emboldens my hands to explore further.

"I don't think you do." I squeeze his middle, deciding to be selfish for once in my freaking life and keep his body close. How often does a girl have a muscled god in her bed? "I don't want you to go."

"Mel…" Tyler gazes down, a cloud of indecision hovering just below the surface. "We don't have to rush."

I chew the inside of my lip. It's decision time. Old stereotypes swirl in my mind. The ones I held before Aaron shredded my heart.

Love before hitting the sack.

Love needs to grow to see a future.

Hell, spending more than a handful of hours with someone before doing the horizontal mambo.

Screw it.

For the first time in my life, I take what I want.

I shove Tyler's shoulder, catching him off guard to move the giant lug to his back. His eyes widen as I straddle his hips. His hands grasping the plushness of my thighs in the skinny jeans I wore to dinner tonight. Nerves jangle as he scans my body, his thumbs moving to stroke the line of my waist. My breath catches. I wish it weren't so damn soft.

What do I expect? It's been ages since I've done a freaking sit up.

Years of self-doubt beats down on me. Every ounce of courage goes into staying where I am. Vulnerable. Even in the dim light.

Good thing Tyler's a thirst trap under my palms, the width and cuts of his torso a distraction. My fingers shake as I work the buttons, but every inch of tan skin revealed boosts my confidence.

"I don't want to talk. I don't want to think about tomorrow. You get credit for being a gentleman. Does that help?"

Chapter Thirteen

Tyler

Does that help?

Does that fucking help?

No! This is such a bad idea.

As good as I want to be, I don't think I have the willpower to turn down this woman. She drives me crazy.

All thoughts of why this is bad dry up as I slide my palms along the rough denim hiding Melanie's curves. Every time that luscious ass wiggles in my lap, my cock stirs. Those jeans tortured me all night. Now's my chance to show this woman exactly how much.

Fire burns through my veins as I curl fingers into her waistband, itching to strip those cock-teasing jeans bare. Only her tense body gives me pause. "Is this okay?"

Melanie nods mutely, her fingertips skimming my belly, searing my skin as I wait. The button on my jeans pops and I groan, fisting the rough fabric at her hips to maintain control. She seems braver when I hold still, but it's goddamn torture.

Her eyes rake over my chest, everywhere her fingers roam. Warmth follows their wake as she traces the path down my abs, nails scraping through the coarse hair on the way to free my tortured cock.

My breath whooshes out, but I still her hands at my zipper. "Wait."

Her pout turns into a seductive vixen when she slides back, those lush hips grinding against the bulge I have no hope of hiding. "I don't want to wait."

"That right?" Letting this sprite of a woman go at her own pace is killing me, but there's no way in hell I'm getting naked first. Standing, I take my little sprite vertical, grinning when Melanie squeals and wraps her thighs tighter to my hips.

"You're going to drop me!"

"Am I?"

To prove a point, I turn toward the bed, holding Melanie's weight in one hand. Her warm center presses to my pained length, and I grind my teeth to hold back. Satiny skin trembles as I snake up her back, under the flimsy cotton to grip her long length of neck.

"Tyler!"

"Yes?" She's spread before me midair like a tasty buffet, and I grin, leaning in to nip at her chin. "Is there something you need?"

"Yes!" Her nails dig into my shoulder. "I need you to put me down."

Giving in, I lay her top half on the bed and roll my hips between those soft thighs. Melanie gasps, drawing me in to catch the sound. I sample from her wine-stained lips, nibbling softly at their plumpness, swallowing her moans. She kisses me as hard as she can while held in my grasp. "Is that better?"

She nods, giving my free hand permission to explore under the loose hem of her shirt. I watch warring emotions flicker across her face until I reach the underside of lace and stop. Frustration wins out and her back arches, offering those glorious breasts on a pedestal. My thumbs trail her ribcage, teasing the edge of pretty fabric while my brain tries to grab ahold of my control.

A text chimes from the nightstand and I pause. "You need to get that?"

"God, no!"

I chuckle, stripping her shirt to get my hands on the breasts I've obsessed over since meeting the scowly woman the first time. "Beautiful."

Melanie's skin pinks over the intricate lace. I bend forward, nibbling at the overflowing mound. The skin slicks under my tongue as I bite, sliding both hands to squeeze the plump flesh together. "God! I love these."

Her raspy laughter vibrates under my lips, ending in a moan when I draw one peaked nipple into my mouth through the lace. She grabs my head, holding it still as I sample and suck raspberries across her flawless skin. "Tyler..."

My name has never sounded sexier.

I need more.

Tugging the cups lower, I rub my scruff across the flawless skin to the place where Melanie's neck curves to shoulder, letting my hands play. Her stiff peaks harden under my palm as I press them together for my lips to explore. Her lemony scent drives me wild, but it's those moans that break my control. Every intake of breath guides my movements. Harder, softer. Swirling my tongue. Nibbling, sucking.

That little eye roll... yes!

"Tyler... more..."

"My pleasure." I lean back, tugging off those tight jeans that stand in my way. "Or yours," I say when she works the corner of her lip.

Backing up, I remove her pants, taking the tiny lace undies with me, and toss them to the side. Part of me wishes she'd stand and model the set for me, but chances are slim. Not with that worried knit in her brow. The way her knees tilt closed with embarrassment.

Growling, I press those knees deeper into the mattress. "Don't hide from me."

A flush works across those soft swells as I slip one of her bra straps lower, down that tantalizing curve of shoulder. Then the other, releasing the strain of those full breasts into my waiting hands. My resolve firms.

"Tonight, I'm making you come. No sex."

She starts. "Wha—"

I capture the argument with my lips before it becomes a full thought. "Will you let me?"

Another text chimes from Melanie's phone as I climb onto the bed and she frowns.

I wait.

The emotions flashing across her face test my resolve to be the good guy. Until her naked pelvis tilts, rubbing her warm middle against my thigh, and my control snaps. I straddle her hips, giving myself full view when I snap the clasp of that lace bra, freeing those perfect mounds.

All focus goes into keeping my touch soft. I bring their plumpness to my mouth, covering the soft flesh with love bites to distract my pained cock. Those sultry whimpers are a lightning rod aiming all blood flow south as her back arches, her wet core wiggling against my lower stomach.

Reaching down, I slide a hand through her wetness, rubbing my knuckles against the little nub buried in her folds. "Tyler... please."

My fingers dive deeper, spreading the moisture across her center, my thumb circling. Her movements become frantic, demanding I move faster. "What do you want, baby girl?"

"I... I don't know."

Those voluptuous hips press higher, telling me without words, and I smile, sliding a finger smoothly inside. A second joins the first, circling her front wall until I find the spot that... "*Ahh!*"

Yes!

That sound.

I pulse over the spot slowly, swallowing every whimper. Capturing every frustrated groan that slips out as her velvety muscles massage my finger. Faster. The heel of my palm strokes the top of her mound on every pass as my thrusts pick up speed. Melanie's nails dig into my back, her moans growing louder.

Shit! She bit my lip!

I bite back a groan, my cock pulsing painfully against my zipper. My forehead falls to hers, drowning in those jade pools. Heat flares as I pinch one strained nipple, tugging it roughly as payback for that bite. She moans. Tight muscles squeezing as her hips riding the waves of my fingers.

"Yes," I growl into her neck. "Give it up, gorgeous." She's almost there.

I bend, suctioning that sweet-smelling spot behind her ear, grinning against her soft skin as her head falls back and comes like a freight train.

Damn... those little gasps as she descends from the high I gave her, those dazed eyes, swell my chest with pride.

I stroke the back of my fingers across her heated cheeks, taking in the beauty of Melanie with defenses down. Pink tinted skin darkens the sprinkle of freckles across her nose. Moist lips part as she pants, teasing me with a peek at that tiny tongue. Unfortunately, our afterglow cuts short by Melanie's ring tone, one that stiffens all the orgasm-relaxed muscles underneath me.

"Ugh!" She shoves at my chest, trying to sit up before I've removed my fingers.

"Hang on, honey." I disentangle, trying not to take offense at the hurried way she climbs off the bed.

"Sonofabitch."

"What is it?" Worry has me at her side in half a second. "Are you okay?" She slams the phone down, ignoring my question as she tries to scuttle past me toward the shirt I tossed on the floor. I grab her wrist, catching Aaron's name flashing from the corner of my eye. "Is he bothering you?"

"What? No!"

Melanie huffs as she tugs her arm free and jerks her bra off the floor, her breasts jiggling as she binds them away from my eyes. She must be upset. She doesn't even try to cover herself or hide from view. The shy girl I stripped less than thirty minutes ago is long gone, replaced with a coiled tiger.

Well, if someone caged that tiger and shook it before letting that tiger free.

"Does he normally call you at night?" My temper flares as I button the bottom of my shirt. My freaking stomach is still warm from her using me as a rubbing post. It tugs at the piece of me missing our post-orgasm cuddle. Something between erupting volcano and ice princess.

Goddamn Aaron.

Daggers hit me the moment her shirt is in place, slapping the questions right out of my mouth. Her arms cross. That venomous stare shriveling my balls. "Not that it's any of your business, but *no*, he doesn't call me every night. I'm sure Aaron wanted to continue where his mother left off tonight."

Her phone vibrates a voicemail against the side table as if calling her a liar. I fold my arms, my stance mirroring hers. "Let me tell that fucker off." She rolls her eyes at my very genuine offer. *Stubborn woman.* "He's got no right to bother you after what he did." A shadow passes over her features, drawing me closer. I lift her chin. "Melanie, every man in this town would love nothing more than to toss his sniveling ass out of it."

The stress knot between my shoulder blades tightens. How I love to nail that equine nose until it's as crooked as a veteran hockey player.

Instead of fixing the downward tilt of her lips, Melanie's frown deepens. "You should go."

My spine jerks straight. "Huh?"

Melanie already has her jeans on and is heading for the door, assuming I'll follow like a good little puppy, and dammit if that isn't what I do.

"It's late," she says, her tone detached, flat. Nothing I say tonight is going to unlock the door that she slammed shut with one fucking phone call.

I said I'd be patient.

Time to man up.

Before I leave though... I stalk toward Melanie's apartment door, where she's waiting to usher me out like her dirty little secret. Bending, I lean close, gripping her chin between my fingers. Fire singes the air between us.

"I will leave... for now. But this isn't the end of this." I mash our lips together in a rough kiss, reminding Melanie of our explosive chemistry with a few deep swipes against her tongue. "Dream of me, baby."

Willpower is at an all-time low, but I force my feet to walk out the door. Melanie's glazed over expression is a welcome replacement to the worry there before. It—and my right hand—will have to hold me over until I get the chance to climb between those delicious thighs again.

Next time for a lot longer.

Chapter Fourteen

Melanie

Figures I'd get behind a massive hay trailer when I'm already running late for dinner at Liza's. It's either karma or bad luck, but today has been a total clusterfuck.

After last night, I woke up guilty as hell. My stomach twists, even now, remembering Tyler's crestfallen expression when I told him to leave. He did nothing wrong.

Hell, he did *everything* right. I've never orgasmed so fast in my life.

Why did I let Aaron mess up something good... again? That man must have a sixth sense for when I'm happy, because he sure knows when to torpedo it.

Today, he's been silent. No more texts. I didn't respond to that chastising tone yesterday, and I never listened to his voicemail, either. Why give him satisfaction?

"Hurry up!" I yell at the giant farm truck, tapping my thumbs along the steering wheel. I'm not about to honk the horn. Blocked two-lane roads are a part of country life.

Only, I've slid into a funk where every step forward I take, there's an alligator pit and an erupting volcano to climb over. Why can't life just be easy? It's certainly smooth for one particular mama's boy I know.

Promising to arrive early to work on our business plans, or whatever idea Liza has to market ourselves as a package deal, sounded great. But by the time I pull down Liza's driveway, frustration has me pricklier than a porcupine. And judging by the cars parked in front of the house, this will not be a quiet hang out night with my friend.

"Great." Grumbling, I stack my purse on the boxed pie I picked up from the bakery. I recognize Lennox's car from the bachelorette party, and Liza's. Two trucks flank the side of the house and my gut sinks when I recognize one of them.

I should have known.

"Here goes nothing," I say to the dimming sky. Wispy pink and purple clouds streak through the orange and blue like painted with Monet's paintbrush. Happier than I feel lifting a hand to knock.

Inside, an awkward dinner awaits with a guy with either a heavily bruised ego, or an epic case of blue balls.

The door opens to Liza mid-laugh, and she tugs me inside, wrapping me in a hug before we're two steps into the living room. "Thank you so much for coming! Smith got so excited when we finished clearing downstairs that he wouldn't wait to have people over."

"It looks amazing."

I mean, I don't know what it looked like before. But other than some wear on the wood floors, you'd never know the place was anything other than a cute farmhouse. Liza has complained about cleaning up after her grandfather's hoarding tendencies, and the awful state of his house since I met her, so this is huge.

"Tyler and Smith have done amazing work. I can clean and trash plenty, but all that rotten wood and broken pipes are out of my ballpark."

Her self-deprecating laugh is hard not to join. "I get it. I can hold my own with a screwdriver and a paintbrush, but power tools... no, thank you."

A sisterly smile lights up her face. "Right!" She takes the pie from my hand and turns for the kitchen, leaving me shuffling my feet in her wake toward the sound of baritone laughter. "Guys, Melanie brought pie."

Four searing brown eyes nail me to my spot.

Smith smirks at Liza, wrapping one sculpted arm around her shoulders and kissing the side of her head. "You know I only eat your pie, baby."

I look away, hiding the surge of jealousy at his sweetness. Only Tyler's knowing gaze catches my breath, leaving me rudderless in the center of the room.

"Hi," he says, his voice thick as molasses.

"Hi."

Liza shoots me a quizzical look from underneath the crook of Smith's arm, which is easier to look at than his smirk.

"Come on, Lenny's out back." Before I can argue about the cold, she has me by the shoulders, ushering me out in front of her. "What was that?" she hisses in my ear.

"Shut. It." Laughing, I shove her off and join Lennox by the firepit. She leans forward for a hug, looking slightly confused. The whiskey in her whip cream topped coffee slaps me in the face. "Damn girl!"

Lennox chuckles and points at the door. "Culprit. Right there."

Tyler is walking our way with two steaming mugs and a cocksure smile. My butt hits the wood log before consciously deciding.

"Ladies, mixed you up some goodies to stay warm." He hands Liza her coffee, before swaggering over to hand me mine. *Is the catwalk effect of Tyler's walk all in my head? Maybe.* "Mel."

My name sounds dirty on his lips and I reach up, taking the cup without meeting those fiery eyes. The mid-February air is not cool enough to deal with Tyler's proximity.

His fingers slide across mine, zinging electricity through my knuckles that remind me of the pleasure those fingers brought last night. He doesn't let go when I have hold of the handle.

My breath catches. "Thank you."

Tyler's entire demeanor softens with his smile. It's as if nothing at all happened last night. "If you hate it, blame Smith." With one wink, the anxiety that's lived in my gut all day evaporates. *Holy hell.*

Once Tyler disappears inside the house, Lennox and Liza lean their heads together. "Oooo…" Their fingers rub together like two little girls playing the *'shame, shame, shame'* game.

"Stop it." I reach behind the log I'm sitting on for a pinecone to toss at their pretty little faces. Well, not right at them. I'd never hurt my friends. Still… they break into a fit of giggles when my lob flies completely over their heads and I can't help but join them.

"What did I miss?" Lennox asks, rubbernecking between me and Liza.

She smirks. "Tyler's been helping our friend move in."

"Hmm, Tyler *is* a helpful person."

Liza cocks her head. "Has Tyler given you the *full* handyman service?"

I narrow my eyes at their mocking tones, but ignore the tease in favor of sipping my delicious Irish Coffee. "If your fiancé had taken care of his apartment, maybe there wouldn't be so much work to do."

Okay... maybe a small jab, but Liza's grin simply widens.

"Smith is a slob. You're not telling me anything." She glances at the back window where Smith and Tyler's silhouettes stand tussling back and forth, their laughter ringing out into the yard. "Except in the kitchen. In there, the man is a genius."

"Shouldn't that be the bedroom?" Lennox asks, elbowing Liza in the ribs.

She snickers. "There too. Hallelujah!"

Lennox lifts her coffee in the air. "Cheers to that."

I lift in solidarity, but honestly, outside of the interrupted encounter last night, I wouldn't say anyone has ever satisfied me in the bedroom.

"What's that face?"

Both women are staring at me when I look up, concern tilting their mouths down. I shake myself. "No face. I'm fine."

"You thinking about Aaron?"

I snort. "God, no! Aaron's sole skill in the bedroom involved snoring louder than a foghorn in San Francisco."

"Good riddance," Lennox grumbles under her breath.

"No kidding." My gaze draws to the house instinctively, cringing over how I acted last night.

As if sensing my thoughts, Tyler's hulking body appears in the doorway. "Dinner, ladies." His eyes fall to mine and hold, the seconds freezing with the temperatures in the air.

"Da-yum," Lennox says, offering a hand to lift me up. "That boy has it bad."

I glance down, hope clogging in my throat. They have no idea what's gone on. How I messed up? Do I try to make things right? Is it too soon?

Lennox links her arm with mine, dragging me with a laughing Liza toward the house. "Whatever worries you've got in that head, girl, forget them. Grab that boy by the balls and make him your bitch."

Liza grows serious. "Tyler is a great man, Mel. Maybe the perfect man to clean your palate after Aaron."

The idea takes root as we find seats in the dining room.

Rustic mason jars center the table. Charcoal placemats and napkins circled with copper accents match the décor. With the soft gray walls, the room is a picture of farmhouse romance. Exactly the style I'd love in a future home.

If I can ever afford one. Let alone the family to put in it.

That thought settles like a bag of rocks in my stomach.

Everyone gravitates to chairs, leaving me right beside Tyler. This will either be exactly what I need, or the most awkward night of my life.

"Hi," Tyler says, pulling out my chair. His fingertips trail my back as he takes his seat, only removing his hand once it becomes obvious we're the center of attention.

Heat rushes my face. "Thanks." I ignore the interested gazes and turn to Lennox for a distraction. "Where's your honey tonight?"

She pouts. "Away game."

"Poor baby," Smith drawls, setting a cast iron pan in the center of the table. Perfectly browned pot roast curves over the top, resting in a bed of sliced carrots and baby potatoes. The thing must be larger than my forearm, and my mouth waters as the savory aroma fills the room.

"That smells delicious!" The entire table leans forward as if runners at the starting line for dinner. If I'm not mistaken, Smith's cheeks turn the lightest shade of pink under his tan.

"It's Liza's favorite," he says, kissing my friend's head as she comes up beside him with a basket of cornbread.

"Thanks, honey."

They take their seats side by side and I feel a surge of relief that our home-style meal will keep the evening casual. So unlike dinners with Aaron's family. I can't thank enough heavens to have these people propping my sanity up right now.

Smith smiles at his fiancée. "We got Melanie's pie for dessert, and Bree sent over a new elevated brownie she's working on for Two-Fourteen."

Liza chuckles. "We're her Guinea Pigs before she puts it on specials à la mode." Fiona slaps her hands on her plastic tray.

"We won't argue about free dessert. Right, Fi?" Lennox lights up, making it impossible not to join the lighter mood of the evening.

If I stop worrying about Tyler. Stop thinking about Aaron.

Smith stands, grabbing the expensive looking carving knife to serve dinner. He passes out thick slices to the ladies first, before fixing his and Tyler's plates. Liza spoons veggies after Lennox holds her plate.

While in Rome.

After everyone has their dinners and Smith takes his seat, conversation gravitates to the repairs completed on the house and what's left on their to do list... It's a lot.

"Did you guys have any bedroom visitors this morning?" Tyler asks, and I lift a brow.

"You guys got a new kink?" Liza smacks Lennox in the shoulder.

"The raccoon, you doof." Lennox chuckles, rubbing her shoulder as she takes a mouthful of carrot.

"Your fix worked great, Ty."

I glance over and Tyler beams, leaning in to not-whisper conspiratorially. "Smith is afraid of furries climbing in his bed."

He scowls at his friend. "Don't know about you, but I don't like things who carry diseases in my bed."

Liza pats his shoulder. "Aww, honey. I let you in my bed."

"Ooo, burn." Echoes Lennox and Tyler. Smith rolls his eyes, but it's easy to join in their laughter, even feeling slightly odd-ball out. The bond between all of them tugs at the part of me left lonely by a childhood traveling to schools across the country. Best friends don't stick when your free-spirited mom hops from job to job, searching for fulfillment.

I feel like a voyeur watching heat flow between Liza and Smith as he leans over and nibbles on the tip of her ear. "I've had all my shots though, baby. And you like my animal side." Smith winks and Tyler groans.

"TMI, man. TMI."

Quietly, I move the food around on my plate, eating small bites here and there as their laughter rolls and Lennox breaks off into venting about on a teacher giving her grief at school. Tyler leans over, his husky voice thick in my ear. "You okay, darlin'?"

Tingles work down the length of my spine. "I'm fine."

Tyler smirks, reminding me of the last time I used that word. "I was happy to see you here."

"Yeah?" My heart kicks into high gear.

"Of course." The earnestness in his eyes makes it impossible to argue. "I planned to stop by after leaving here, anyway."

I swallow around the nerves pushing up at his nearness. "After last night?"

A mischievous smile tilts his lips. "I'm not scared easily." Reaching over, his hand lands on the top of my knee, squeezing. "Good things are worth fighting for."

My jaw falls slightly before I remember I'm supposed to be eating dinner and jerk forward, forking an overeager bite of beef into my mouth. Anything to keep from answering the challenge in his voice.

Tyler chuckles and sits forward to his own meal with a wink. Liza offers me a soft smile that I return, praying my face isn't the color of a lobster.

Smith clears his throat. "So, we love having you guys over to christen the dining room, but there's another reason we wanted to get together tonight."

Liza's grin cracks wide and she grabs Smith's hand. The baby quiets, fascinated by her parents talking. "You guys know how we're redoing the house, obviously. My gramps left us, uh... quite a project here."

"A pricey one," Smith adds.

"We couldn't have come close to where we are without Tyler. Without your work and time..." She shakes her head, smiling at the man beside me with such affection. He looks taken aback.

He waves her off. "You guys are doing me a favor, too."

"Yeah, but without your help, Ty, it would take forever to get to this point." Smith looks at his daughter. "We want to get settled fast... for Fi."

"And speaking of getting settled..." Liza looks at Smith, a secret glowing in her eyes. "Smith and I are planning a sort of... elopement."

"Ahh!" Lennox and I squeal, hopping up and circling the table to wrap Liza in a hug sandwich. Congratulations mingle into chaos at the table, baby Fiona clapping her cute little hands in celebration with the adults. Tyler slaps Smith's back, whispering something in his ear that has Smith pulling his best friend in harder.

"It's going to be up at North Slopes, but we want you guys there with us." Smith glances around, warmth shining in his dark brown eyes when he sees Liza's giant smile. "We're gonna drive up with Fiona and my dad." He claps Tyler on the shoulder. "I hope you'll be my best man?"

"Dude! You ask anyone else and I'm cutting your balls off!" Excitement radiates off Tyler as he bounces from foot to foot, looking like a kid in a candy store. "So proud of you, man," he whispers, pulling Smith into another back-slapping hug.

"Thanks, Ty. We aren't doing anything fancy. No walking down the aisle shit."

"Yeah," Liza says. "I don't have any family left, other than you guys. Doing something big in town just didn't feel right." Smith wraps his arms around her shoulders.

"We didn't want any walk down the aisle weirdness, or all those eyes staring at us."

A watery laugh slips out, my heart bottoming out at the talk of wedding plans. It wasn't long ago, I canceled my pomp and circumstance. My mom would have walked me down the aisle, even without approving of the relationship, but now I know, if I ever plan to get married, it will not be dressed as a creampuff in front of people who care more about the caliber of steak served that the love being vowed in front of them.

Liza turns to me and Lennox. "Would you ladies be my Maid-of-Honor and Bridesmaid?"

"Oh, my god! Of course!" Lennox screeches, clapping her hands in excitement.

Fiona joins her with the most adorable baby giggle. I can't help but sweep a hand over her dewy, partially grown in hair. "I'd love to, Liza. Thank you so much for thinking of me." I glance up to find Tyler staring at me with a funny look on his face.

Before I can unravel the exposed feeling I have around this man, Liza rushes around the table and wraps me in a comforting hug that steals a bit of my anxiousness over the reminder of wedding bells. The memory of all the planning is too fresh.

"And don't worry, eloping means none of the Bridezilla stuff. We lucked into a cancelation at the resort at the end of the month, so we're just going to do it." Smith's warm gaze mirrors her giddiness. As much as a stoic military man can, I guess.

"So, what can we do? How do we help?" Lennox asks, taking her cell phone out of her purse and opening the notes app.

"Nothing," Liza says, returning to her seat. "I'm serious that we have it all taken care of. I found this sweet lace number from the shop. Smith will wear his dress blues, but that's about as formal as we'll get." She beams at Smith like the hero he is and I can't help but flick over to Tyler.

What does he look like in his dress uniform?

Holy hell!

He catches me staring and smiles, reaching over again to squeeze my knee.

"I'll grab dessert." Smith leaves the room while Liza fills everyone in on the hotel deal they found. Third night free when booking two. A tiny chapel plucked right off a Swiss mountainside.

Simple flowers are provided, chocolate-covered strawberries in their honeymoon suite, and there's a restaurant on-site for us all to enjoy after the I-do's.

"All you guys need to do is request off work the last weekend this month. Maybe Friday too, if you can swing it."

"No problem," we echo as Smith sits the most delicious smelling brownie right in front of me. My mouth waters. "Don't need to worry about time off." I chuckle. "My boss is kinda a bitch, though."

"Oh, stop." Liza waves away my joke, spooning a tiny portion of chocolate onto Fiona's plate. The baby girl immediately sets to paint it all across her high chair, occasionally sucking her fingers with the sweetest grin on her lips.

"I'll book my room when I get home today. This is so exciting," I say, realizing I actually am. For all my hangups over men right now, I see the devotion between Liza and Smith when they look at each other. After all the pain in their past, I'm over the moon to be a part of their happy future.

Over dessert, we hear more about the boutique ski lodge and Liza's guilt over not using our love-obsessed little town for her wedding. I've never been skiing, but the more she talks, the more my excitement grows. By the time the evening is done, I have a mental list rolling of gear I need to buy or rent on the mountain, and a plan for organizing the few small details this week with Liza and Lennox when we meet up for dinner.

It takes monumental effort to leave before everyone else, but I can't talk to Tyler yet. Not when my thoughts are a jumbled mess around him. If I had taken his offer to walk me to my car, I know I would have given in and kissed his face off. The man has heavenly lips and damn sure knows how to use them. After hours of his rich, masculine scent tempting me more than the prime rib Smith cooked, there's no way I could deny anything he requested.

And I can't risk that.

Not yet.

Chapter Fifteen

Tyler

The phone behind the register jars me out of yet another wishful daydream about the beautiful pixie not a block down the road.

"Jackson's Hardware. How can I help you?"

"Good afternoon. I'm calling because it appears your car warranty is due to expire in thirty days. I wanted to explain our current special running, so you won't be left with lapsed coverage."

A loud guffaw slips out before I school my expression.

"Is that right?" Somehow, I doubt my truck, who's older than I am, recently expired for any sort of coverage. I bought the thing off my grandpa when I was sixteen and had Axel restore its engine a few years ago. Best truck I've ever driven.

"Absolutely, sir. The last thing you want is to blow a gasket without proper coverage. We have a low interest payment plan if needed. Would you like to hear our specials?"

"I'm going to blow a gasket all right. Why don't you stop trying to scam people with fake warranties?" I slam the phone back to the cradle, irrationally annoyed that the phone call wasn't the one I've waited for all morning.

After last night's dinner and Melanie's abrupt ending to Saturday night, I assumed she wouldn't welcome an early morning wake up call. "I sent muffins, dammit." Okay, there was also a bottle of champagne that I wish I could share with her. Gary confirmed their delivery at 8 a.m., and I don't want to admit that I've waited on pins and needles since.

"Anything important?" Dad's voice rises from the back of the store where he and a few of the neighborhood cronies sit gossiping about the town.

"Nah. Junk call." A round of raucous laughter rings from the back, my father's curiosity satisfied. "I'm taking my lunch," I shout, already locking the register. Dad will hear the bells over the door if a customer enters. If I don't get some air soon, though, I'll be about as useful as a blunt saw blade.

Outside, I beeline for the diner, letting the sun warm my face for the short walk instead of driving. I'm too fidgety to sit in a truck, but the Hope's hungry man country-fried steak hits the spot when my skin feels too itchy, like today. Call it indulgent, but when I work outside sixteen-hour days, sustenance is important.

Who am I kidding? Frequenting the diner when the hungry man is on the menu is all about comfort.

My mama also used to cook the best country-fried steak this side of the Dixon, and Hope's is close enough to remind me of Ma's comfort. With one confusing female tying me up in knots, I need something satisfying to boost my patience. A man's pride can only take so much before he feels like a love-sick puppy dog.

How can I convince Melanie to take a chance so soon? Her asshole ex broke her trust. I get it. I just don't like it.

Ideas roll in my head as I turn the corner for the diner, but the sight unfolding in the middle of the sidewalk stops me in my tracks. Melanie stands, shoulders stiff, face molten red as she shoves her loose curls out of it. Aaron's hands swing wildly, whatever trash he's spewing more agitated and in Melanie's face than I like.

"You need to go." Melanie's voice hitches and I start across the road.

"You'd rather live in this shit hole? What's wrong with you?" Aaron's tone lights a match under my heels and I'm at her side before that dumbass utters another word.

"What the fuck you think you're doing?"

He rolls his eyes, focusing on Melanie. "Your bulldog sounds cranky? You might wanna spend less time on your little business and give him a treat every now and again." He snickers. "Maybe if you gave me more treats, I wouldn't have looked elsewhere for them."

"You fucker." Growling, I grip the stuffy lapels at Aaron's chest in my fist and twist, shoving his sniveling spine against the brick wall behind me. The shock on his face gives me a moment of satisfaction until that thin lip curls to the side, a malicious smile morphing his ugly face into something sinister.

Anger surges and I rip Aaron off the wall, slamming his weight with enough force that his head knocks the wall. Oops.

Leaning forward, I lock eyes with the coward, who thinks screaming at a woman on the street is okay. Flashbacks of the same scrawny fucker tossing my books in the lunchroom because I had a secondhand backpack spur my anger. "You're a coward, Aaron. Haven't you realized that?" I step back, giving the man space before I do something that gets me in trouble.

He shoves off, straightening his blazer. The crumbles of brick clinging to his shoulders satisfy at least the part of me that wants to dirty this boy up. If I can't beat his preppy face in.

"You wanna call off Fido over here?"

"Woof!"

Melanie slaps my chest, ignoring Aaron. "As much as I'd love to watch you dirty him up, he's not worth it."

"I'm not worth it? Hah!" Aaron's face goes molten red. "You're lucky I offered you the chance to come back." He straightens his shoulders. "You were a frigid prude, anyway."

"Do you think a real man blames a woman for his weakness?" I stalk forward. "But you're not a real man, are ya, Aaron? You know what? Your loss is my gain."

Curious eyes peek through Klassy Kuts, cutting off my argument. The last thing Melanie needs is this scene spreading through the gossip mill.

"Fuck off, country boy."

"Tyler, let's go!" She pulls at my elbow, her soft hands warm on my bare arms. Lunch is long forgotten, but her pained eyes move me a few steps down the sidewalk.

Tucking Melanie into my side feels decadent. That she lets me swells my pride, and I grin. "You don't have to worry about

Melanie anymore, Aaron. She's in *really* good hands." I wiggle my fingers in the air, insinuating everything I can't wait to do to Melanie again.

"Tyler!" My name is a hiss on those beautiful lips, but she doesn't wait for me. Melanie is out from under my arm without so much as a backward glance, her annoyed grumbles trailing behind her as she turns the corner to the back entrance of her apartment.

"Ooo, trouble in paradise. You should let that one go, Tyler. Find yourself one of these little bumpkins to warm your bed."

"Mother-fu—" Aaron scoots around the BMW I didn't notice parked on the street before I can pound his face in. I pull on every ounce of self-control in my body to walk away with a two-bird salute and head for Melanie's apartment. This asshole is obviously still bothering her. We're going to have a serious conversation about getting that man away from her permanently.

My pace picks up, but by the time I round the corner, Melanie is out of sight. "Great." My stomach grumbles that no lunch is coming, but I've got a few important things to do first.

Taking the back stairs two at a time, I hurry, needing to make sure Melanie is okay. It's a tremendous effort to keep the urgency out of my knock, but the last thing I need is to anger her anymore.

"Go away!"

"You didn't ask who it was."

The door cracks open. "Don't care. Both of you can go away."

She goes to slam the door, but I put my foot in the way, thankful for steel-toe boots. "I just want to check on you."

Green eyes roll to the ceiling, her head falling to the door as if she's lost the energy to deal with me. "I'm tired Tyler. Why don't you just listen to Aaron and go after another girl? I'm a waste of time."

My throat catches. "What the fuck!" Rage pushes thoughts of going slow or being gentle to the wayside. I shove the door, careful not to hit Melanie as I step inside. Her eyes bulge, but she doesn't look scared, so I step closer. "You, my lady, made a mistake." She blinks, straightening her shoulders like she's ready to fight. Good. Spunk is better than sadness.

When she opens her mouth to argue, I press a finger there, bending to hover close to the scent of her fruity shampoo. "Never repeat the trash out of that fool's mouth." Leaning my hand against the wall, I lock eyes, willing her to let me in. "You are beautiful, and as far as I know, sweet as Minnie's pie."

A soft blush darkens those freckled cheeks. I drop a kiss to one side, tracing the other side with my thumb.

Her breath hitches. "Tyler, you don't know me."

I pull back to search those green depths, trapping her face so she can't look away. "I know enough. I know I want to take you out. I know you need to forget everything that asshole ever said to you." Melanie's eyes sparkle, ramping up my need to fix the things Aaron broke. Unable to stop myself, I drop a kiss to the corner of her downturn lips, knowing she could push me away any minute.

Those plump lips part, sucking in a quick breath that pushes her breasts against my chest. *God, what I'd give to pull her in tighter.* I wait, though, needing Melanie to give me the go ahead after her hesitancy for an actual relationship.

She turns until we're nose to nose, lips a hairbreadth from touching. Her eyes burn fire, questioning as she scans my face. "You say such… things. I don't know if I should pinch myself to wake up or slap you because you have to be playing a game."

"No games. I don't play, honey. Not with women and not with your feelings." I drop my forehead to hers. "Melanie, if I got you in my bed, I'd show you how a real man takes care of his woman."

"Yes."

I jerk back. "Yes?" A light of excitement turns her eyes into a spring meadow dancing in the wind. "Yes to what, Mel? Spell it out real clear for me, baby."

"You. Everything you just said." She tries to look away, but I loop a finger under her chin, keeping her gorgeous eyes on me. I need to read her, and I've met no one with expressive eyes like this one. "I want... I want to feel alive. The way you make me feel."

A giant grin splits my face as I lift Melanie by the backs of her thighs, squeezing the supple flesh in my hands. I can't wait to get her bare, but I want her to know I love the curves Aaron made fun of. Sweet thighs that beg for my fingerprints.

"Tyler!" she gasps. "I'm too heavy."

"You're perfect. Shut up." I swat her backside, pulling an excited squeal from those lips before I latch on, pressing Melanie's spine to the wall. Her breast flatten to my chest as our tongues explore, sipping, testing. Melanie chases my lips as I pull back, leaving barely an inch between us. Her panting breaths tease my cheek, silently begging for more. More I plan to give, but first to wash these degrading thoughts from her head. It's no wonder Aaron never got her off. I won't make the same mistake. Nipping at her bottom lip, I swallow a whimper, pausing when she tries to deepen the kiss further. "What did I tell you about putting yourself down?"

A shy smile tilts the corner of her lips. "Don't do it?"

"Damn right, don't do it." To prove my point, I shift Melanie's weight into one hand, curling the other around her back to cup a handful of silky curls as her strong thighs squeeze my middle. "Does this feel like I have a problem with anything right now?"

She sighs. "No…"

My grin spreads as I trail my scruff along the soft skin of her jaw, moving to suction the tender skin below her ear. I crave that shiver that works through her supple body over a little rough caress. The way she opens up, chin tilting to the ceiling as I hold her head in place and melt into her warmth.

The press of my zipper becomes too painful. I need room to maneuver.

With my mouth suctioning bites along that sweet tendon that makes Melanie wiggle in my arms, I turn, making quick work of the small distance to her bedroom. The door bounces off the wall as I shove through. If there's any damage, I'll fix it later. Right now, I slowly lower her back to the bedspread and straighten, taking in the raven curls spread across the soft fabric, the panting breaths straining Melanie's t-shirt and giving me tempting views over the v-neck.

"Beautiful," I murmur, leaning forward for a nibble at the exposed flesh. A vein peeks from the top, running along her smooth skin. I trace it with my tongue, squeezing the supple flesh with both hands. The little buds harden under my thumbs and I move to latch onto one through the skirt, grinding my erection against the bed for a little relief. Moving to the other side, I let her sounds guide me. Harder. Softer. A pinch. A squeeze. All of it gets some reaction.

Her hands grip my head as I rip her shirt over her head, exposing another thick lace bra. This one ties around her neck and I smile, tracing the line down the middle, between her ribcage toward the waistband of the too-tight leggings. Bending, I nibble kisses along her ribcage and rid everything hiding her lower half in one swoop.

She squeaks and I grin against her skin, loving how her legs circle my waist again, keeping me close. "Tyler..." My hair tugs almost painfully as I reach her hip bone. I bite, aiming to leave a little momento from our time together. "Tyler, now. No teasing." She pants, and I almost give in.

Desperate hangs tug at my shirt and I give it to her, ripping the thing over my head for a little relief. I'm not going out that easy, though, and I fear when it gets right now too it, I'll come like a teenager who's hot for teacher. Can't have that. I adjust myself, popping my top button as I drop to my knees beside the bed.

"Tyler!"

Ignoring her tugs at my shoulders, I dive into her center, lapping at the wetness like the love-sick puppy I feel around her. Her groan fuels my exploration as I hold her knees apart, swiping her crease once, twice, kneading her inner thighs as I circle the bud at the top. Her back arches and I pull it between my lips, lathing it gently in a figure eight. The scent of her arousal fills my nostrils and I speed up my effort, licking, sucking.

"God! Ty!"

Moaning, I spread her lower lips, dipping my tongue into her channel for a taste. She quivers and I repeat, going deeper, pulling sweet animalistic sounds from Melanie that are going to drive me up a wall. I prop her knee on my shoulder and bury a thumb in her tight channel, my hand spreading her ass as I pulse in time with my lips on her clit. Her hips tilt, taking me deeper and I hum, vibrating in just the right time to rock this beauty over the edge.

"Oh my god! Shit... shit... shit... Tyler!"

Her walls clamp down on my thumb, pulsing as I lap at her wetness, keeping my tongue soft as I pump, drawing out her orgasm.

When she sags to the bed, breath sawing out of her lungs, I climb back over that gorgeous body, thankful she's forgotten her shyness after the first orgasm. I rake the loose curls from her face and smile at the contentment relaxing her face. Those lips, parted as she catches her breath, call to me and I drop a kiss there, grinning when her eyes pop open. I bet she tastes herself on me. It makes me want to dirty her up more.

"Thank you."

My eyebrows must hit my hairline because she chuckles and takes my face in her hands. Her kiss is relaxed, indulgent in the sensual swipe of her tongue against mine. Tasting another person has never lit me up inside like this. I've never been desperate to crawl inside someone and lock us together in sleep.

Melanie's hands travel my shoulders, my chest. She strokes across the muscles in my stomach and I flex for her, pushing my erection into her thigh.

"Naked. Now." She tugs at my zipper, working to slide my pants over the very painful, very in-the-way erection.

"Are you sure?" A huff of frustration hits my neck just before she latches on, suctioning hard as she pulls me on top of her, her heels sliding my pants the rest of the way down my legs. My hips have a mind of their own with her mouth against my neck.

Shit! That's my weakness.

"Tyler Jackson, you better get inside me right now or I'm going to think you're all talk, no show."

I chuckle and tug her head back, capturing her lips before I sit up and remove my boxers. The tiny drop of her jaw is a steroid shot to the ego, and I swear my cock grows even more.

"Condom? Anything in my wallet is going to be old enough to look like Swiss cheese."

She cocks her head curiously as she bites the lip plump from our kisses. "You really aren't having a different woman every weekend, are you?"

I shake my head, wrapping a fist around my cock and giving it a good pull. "Woman, I had to get you off first, because I'm afraid of blowing the moment I bury into that sweet pussy. You've tormented this poor guy since I met you."

Her soft laughter warms me inside as she reaches forward, a soft blush creeping up her neck as she replaces my hand on my cock. My breath catches with the first stroke, a tremor working through my body as she slides base to tip, one hand smoothing across my stomach as she glances up.

"I'm on birth control, Tyler. I told Aaron I wanted to build my business before babies."

I swallow. *Is she saying?*

"I'm clean," I say, diving my fingers into the nape of her hair.

"Me too. I tested twice after that a-hole, just to be sure."

Scanning her eyes, I wait for Melanie to change her mind. Our breaths mingle in the silent bedroom, but when she says nothing, I stretch her back down, covering her body with mine. Every soft curve contours to my hard muscle. Her smooth thigh sliding to hook around my hip.

"No more thoughts of him."

Chapter Sixteen

Melanie

*D*on't think about Aaron… No worries about that.

Not with six feet of hunky muscle pressing me into the mattress.

"Tyler…" I grab his scruff, pulling that smooth-talking mouth in. "Kiss me."

Those striking brown eyes flash before our lips clash in a fever, hands and fingers digging everywhere within reach. I arch, my nipples pebbling against his smattering of chest hair, setting me on fire. My nerves are a jangled mess. My hips tilting, rubbing the needy ache below against his muscled thigh.

Tyler groans, sliding a hand under my ass to hold it against him, grinding in the sexiest dance. My head falls back, panting as I hold on for dear life. Excitement builds until I can barely hold still. The suctioning kisses Tyler drops along my neck short circuit every nerve ending in my body.

"Tyler... now." Tugging at those muscular shoulders, I wrap my legs around that thick waist, desperate to get this show on the road before I come on his leg like a horny Chihuahua. His thick waist, but the sore muscles tomorrow will be worth it if the man lives up to the game he talks.

That impressive rod rests against my curls and Tyler smiles. "Impatient, huh?"

He pulls back, coating his length in my wetness before pushing forward again. Each stroke nudges my clit and I almost scream, digging my nails into his lower back to urge him inside me. I tilt harder than my lower abs have ever worked, silently begging as I lean up to nibble the scruff along his sharp jawline.

Tyler jerks up, bracing a hand by my head that flexes that delicious bicep close enough to bite. So I do. The growl that rumbles in Tyler's chest spurs me on and I wrap my fingers around the eagle tattooed over an American flag there, squeezing as the head of his cock nudges my entrance.

His other hand dives into the back of my hair, tugging back to hold my eyes. "You want me bare, baby?" The promise shining in those dark depths has me nodding before I can change my mind.

He bends, dropping to his elbow and stroking loose hair out of my face. A piece of the ice protecting my heart since Aaron chips away.

Tyler's lips capture mine as his cock spreads me wide, sheathing himself halfway in one smooth thrust. I gasp and Tyler catches it in his mouth, holding me close as he slides out to the tip again. He presses in again, this time animalistic sounds coming from both of us, hot and raw.

"Mel..."

Our hips meet in the middle for a glorious dance that sends a surge of wetness to my core, every movement more intense than the last. Stroke after decadent stroke, Tyler's perfect cock hits that spot inside and my eyes roll back in my head. My nails scrape his back. "Tyler... yes. Harder!"

His head dips, nipping at my ear. "You need more?" he asks, grinding down low like a Ludacris song plays in his head. I groan, tossing my head back against the massive hand holding me in place. There's so much man. So many muscles, I have to touch everywhere.

Tyler's forehead drops to mine, filling my vision as his hips roll, picking up speed. Our tongues battling, ramping the desperation I've fought every second around this man.

"Shit!" I hold on for dear life, flexing and clinging to Tyler as a ball of tension builds below, tiny pulses triggered with every glide of his magnificent cock. *God! If I knew what I was missing before!*

I'm so freaking close.

Tyler must sense it, because one of his callused hands slides to cup my breast, pinching the nipple and bringing it to his mouth. His teeth tease, shooting a jolt of electricity down my spine, and I cry out, legs tightening on his hips.

"Tyler! Oh... god!" Every muscle seizes, tossing me over the edge, and I scream, riding the gold medal of orgasms as I cling to Tyler's dense muscle. He growls, that super control snapping as he bears up on one arm, nearly bending me in half to pound us both against the mattress. It bounces, rubbing my sensitive nipples against Tyler's chest and extending the pleasure.

The sounds of slapping skin mingle with our pants and I slide my hands to the globes of his ass, squeezing that sexiness against me. His strokes grow longer, deeper, until I feel like I'm going to break in half.

Finally, Tyler shudders, his body going rigid as his cock swells. He moans my name, spurting a warmth inside me I've never felt before. I don't know why I gave Tyler permission, but he feels right.

"Holy shit, woman." His weight falls heavy, burying me into the bed, and I grunt. "Crap, sorry." Tyler pulls out, resting his hip on the bed at my side with a laugh.

I sift my fingers through the flop of hair falling across his forehead, enjoying the afterglow of peace. "That was…"

"Yeah." His arms pull me in, squeezing around my middle to keep our bodies flush as we pant for normal breaths. "That's not what I expected for my lunch break today."

I laugh. "A nooner? Can't say I've had one of those before."

"I'd give up Minnie's pie every day for it." He drops a kiss to my shoulder, his hands roaming the outer edge of my hip. "Only one problem, though."

I tense, waiting for the regret, or the *no strings* talk.

Tyler chuckles, one hand moving up to cup my face. "I feel you getting all in your head. Stop it." His lips stop any argument on my lips. Their soft warmth steals the vulnerability of lying here naked with his cum leaking out of me. "All I was going to say is, I'm starving. And while I want to lie naked with you and repeat the last thirty minutes for the next five hours, I need to feed you and me both."

I scoff, but the knot in my chest loosens slightly. "You don't need to feed me." Pushing at his shoulder, I try to slide out from under his distracting weight, but he tugs me tighter.

"Where were you headed when I walked up?"

"To the printers." He squints his eyes. "And I was going to run by the store to grab stuff for lunch. I haven't had time to shop this week."

"Okay, so obviously I distracted you." I smack his shoulder at that smug smile and he pulls back, dropping one last kiss to my shoulder before hopping out of the bed with way more agility than I could muster after the workout we just had.

He disappears into the bathroom and I starfish on the bed, assuming Tyler needs time to clean up. I know I could. Sweat collects at my hairline—and every freaking where.

Gah! I must look like a nightmare walking! Okay, laying, but still. I dig my fingers in my hair and exhale, listening to the water run through the bathroom door. My entire body is on fire. The beard burn along my neck. My nipples. The ache in my inner thigh muscles... freaking lumberjack-sized man.

Despite the soreness in unmentionable areas—hallelujah—my mind is surprisingly at peace. I bit the bullet.

I'd been with Aaron so long, and most of it unhappy, I feel like I ripped off a Band-Aid.

And God, the freaking ripped Band-Aid it was.

A sigh slips out. No matter what happens, I can't regret letting Tyler in.

The bed dips and my eyes fly open, catching Tyler's eyes trailing my legs. I curl up to a sitting position, fighting the flush of embarrassment as I grab the comforter to cover my nakedness. Tyler tsks.

"What do you think you're doing?"

"Uh..." I look down, my jaw dropping when Tyler pulls the comforter away.

"Melanie, I've had my mouth all over you. Don't hide those gorgeous curves from me."

"Stop..." Laughing, I shove at his chest, intending to get up and out of his very attentive line of sight, but Tyler presses on my shoulder, setting me down with a lingering kiss. I close my eyes, but a warm rag smoothing over my middle pops them open again.

"Shh, be still." Tyler kisses me again, cleaning my inner thighs and folds with such gentleness, tears burn my eyes.

When he's done, he tosses the rag in my hamper in the corner and holds out a hand to help me off the bed. I stare at it a second, unable to believe this guy is real. Real and in my life, my bedroom.

Finally, I accept the help and climb down, allowing Tyler to wrap those brawny arms around my waist. He kisses my temple and I stand on my toes, wrapping my arms around his neck for a proper kiss. His cock hangs between us, still somehow half hard with my breast smooshed to his chest. It's hard not to sink into the kiss when his hand spans my back, pressing me close. Somehow, standing here buck naked feels more intimate than what we did before.

"Let's go eat," he says gently, waiting.

"You fed me this morning, and I forgot to say thank you."

"Well, let me feed you again, and you can thank me again later." A playful grin lights his face and I suck in a breath, giving into whatever this is, for however long it is.

"Okay. Let's go."

Chapter Seventeen

Tyler

Rain beats down on my windshield outside of Liza's farmhouse. I hit my steering wheel.

"Damn!" Where the hell are my supplies?

Reaching for my phone, I dial the lumberyard outside of Lexington, getting hotter and hotter as I listen to the ringtone chime. This is going to put me so far behind. Betty needs a hot water heater installed tomorrow. Her's won't hold a pilot light, and I've had one too many phone calls at sunrise when the little old lady wakes up for her morning routine of collecting eggs, feeding her pig, and cleaning up with a preferably not cold shower.

"Lexington Lumber. This is Jessi." The lilting voice on the other end of the line cools my irritation. It's not Jess's fault some delivery dude hasn't finished his route.

"Hey Jess. Do you have an ETA on my delivery?"

"Ty?"

"Yeah, hun. I'm sitting in front of the house and nothing's here yet. I thought John said I'd be first off the truck today, so I can get a jump start on the weekend. I dropped a boatload of reclaimed wood off last week to secure my spot."

"That man's a sucker for some shiplap," she says, laughing.

I snort. "Yeah, me too. And I gave it up to get priority delivery." Fingernails clack against a keyboard, mixing with the sound of the rain against the truck's roof.

"Let me check. Hang on..."

I take a deep breath, focusing on the solace that I wouldn't be able to work in this rain, anyway. Just, Stone has a habit of booking weeks out with the recent lumber shortage and I was very particular with my order.

"I see what happened," she says, coming back on the line. "Notes say we canceled your order earlier this week."

"What!" My shout drowns out the rain and I jerk open the console, pulling out the pack of gum I keep on hand for when I'm anxious. "Why the hell would Stone cancel my order?"

She clacks away again, humming into the phone while she searches, and I fight the urge to scream and shout my irritation.

"Oh, right here! Looks like someone called. Said you didn't need your delivery, and you'd call back with an edited order."

"The fuck?" I say before I can stop myself. "Who the hell would cancel my order?"

"Uh... Stone spoke with him, so I can't say exactly, but the notes say it was Edward, your assistant."

"I don't have an assistant, Jess." My hand slaps the wheel, taking my frustration out on the hard plastic, so I don't say something I'll regret to the sweet receptionist. Stone would have my ass, and with him being the closest lumber supply to town, I don't want to burn that bridge.

"What the... hang on, Ty. Let me check a few things."

Muzaq fills my ears, and I groan, hopping out of the truck. I need to move before I explode. Rain pelts my face, the chill in the air a relief from my rising temper. *Who the hell would mess with my order?* It doesn't make sense.

Moving to the back of the truck, I untuck the tarp and lift the cans of primer I brought for after construction. I hold the phone to my ear as I rush up the stairs, two at a time, dropping the cans under the window, away from the rain. There are only a few supplies I can unpack without lumber. I won't leave my nail gun, or my compressor. Too much risk. All that's left is the bucket of filler and exterior coat. The stash under the window feels inadequate.

I sigh, slinging the hair out of my face, flattened by the rain.

"Ty!" Stone's gruff greeting interrupts his horrible hold music.

"Yeah, man. What the hell is going on?"

"Jess told me what's going on. I don't know what to tell you on our end. Your assistant called a few days ago and said you lost the project and no longer needed the giant order. I warned him the stack was already prepped. We could only refund half with the late cancellation. He said that would be okay."

"*The fuck?* When have I ever canceled last minute? Let alone been okay eating the money, dude. I've ordered from you for years!"

"I know. I know, man. I thought it was odd, but the guy had details of your order and the delivery address. I assumed it was some bad luck that the job fell through. It happens..."

"Yeah, shit happens, but I would be the one calling you." I shake my head, climbing up into the truck for protection from the chill to figure this shit out. "Never mind, man. When can you get the shipment here? I planned to start today, but I can move my schedule around and start tomorrow or Saturday."

"Uh… sorry, Ty. We fulfilled another back order who had waited a few weeks, too."

My brain stalls. "What the fuck you mean, Stone?"

"We sold it. There's a backlog, man."

The steering wheel creaks under my fists. "Stone, I waited five weeks for the lumber…" I trail off, biting off the litany of cuss words that won't earn me any favors. "What am I supposed to do now, Stone? Like seriously?"

"I'm sorry, Tyler. I'll submit your order now."

Worry tightens in my chest. "How long, man?"

There's a long enough pause that kicks up my nerves.

"Tyler, I know this was a fuck up somewhere, but I'm still at the whim of the distributors. I'll submit right now and make a few phone calls. It won't be quick though. I wish it were."

"*Fuck!* Call me as soon as you know."

I hang up, frozen in the cab of my truck. The windows have fogged during the phone call, blurring the sight of my buddy's house. I dread telling him of the delay with everything going on. Settling Fiona into a solid home is their top priority. I feel like I let him down.

Cranking the ignition, I put the truck in gear, dreading having to make that phone call. Without the job this afternoon, I need to figure out a game plan. I have to get back to the store and make some calls. I was hoping to have time to take Melanie to *Two-Fourteen* this weekend.

A text chimes on my way back that I wait until Pop's parking lot to check.

Melanie: Thank you for the Daisies this morning. :)

I smile. Seeing Melanie's name cracks the tension tightening my chest.

Me: Any time, love. Glad you like them.

Me: Dinner Friday?

I see bubbles appear and disappear a few times. Finally, I collect my wallet and rush through the rain, my phone vibrating in my pocket as I make it in the store. I wave at the nineteen-year-old kid working the register. "Where's Dad?"

He barely acknowledges my presence, pointing to the back of the store and I follow, checking my text.

Melanie: Aren't you tired of me yet?

I may have stopped by once or twice. Or three times this week.

Me: Never. Be ready for me tomorrow. 7PM.

Melanie answers with a wink emoji and a salsa girl in a dancing red dress and I'm stuck imagining those dark curls tumbling down the back of a sexy red dress with a plunging neckline as I walk up on my father. I shake my belt a little, discreetly giving my cock a little breathing room before greeting my dad.

"Hey, Pop, you get the hot water heater in yet for Mrs. B?"

He looks up from the box of roofing nails he's unpacking on the shelf and smiles the fatherly smile that never fails to give me comfort. "Yeah, came in this morning. I thought you'd be at the farm this afternoon."

I scoff. "Yeah, me too. Change of plans. Now, I've gotta re-arrange the next few days to be ready for the lumber delay."

"Shew... That sucks, son. Anything I can do."

"Nah. I'll let you know. Right now, it's just an extra pain in my ass."

He chuckles. "I get that. By the way, town hall called for you earlier. I told them you were out."

I glance at my watch. "Shit, they're closed now. I'll have to call them tomorrow." Our town enjoys those 4 p.m. closing hours most days. Unless someone makes an appointment, there's no point in the few employees to keep the office open to stare at the mini-blinds.

"Should I be expecting the sheriff to pop up sometimes?" he asks, chuckling at his own joke as he slaps my shoulder and I roll my eyes.

"One time, Dad. One time."

"Yeah, well, give me a warning to collect bail if you decide to joyride people's sheep anytime soon."

His laughter is infectious, and I can't help but join in as I write down the list of supplies I need for the plumbing repair. "Smith and I were fourteen, Dad. Statute of limitations on that joke."

He snorts, shaking his head. "Still funny."

I finish gathering my toolbox while Dad goes back to humming through his inventory and I set out to get a jump start on Betty's repair, feeling slightly lighter after talking to my dad and setting a real date, our first date, with Melanie.

Chapter Eighteen

Melanie

After Tyler's text yesterday, and all his sweet deliveries this week, I knew I needed to stop by my storage locker to dig out some of my better clothes. I've cleared the boxes I came from Aaron's mom's with, but nothing in there fits the mood of a first date. Especially one with a sexy, non-stick-up-his-ass man.

It's been too many months since I've been this excited, and hopeful, going into a weekend. This afternoon, I've got a meeting at the bookstore to go over some marketing plans. Then, Liza is meeting me to check out a few shops in town. A little combo wedding prep and my own date prep, in case I can't find the dress I'm looking for.

When I catch my mirror in the rearview mirror, the smile crinkling the corner of my eyes surprises the hell out of me. Bouncing a little in my seat, I turn the radio up, singing an old Miley Cyrus song I used to enjoy back in college.

The sun is shining.

My mind is clear.

For the first time since I moved, I feel truly free.

As I turn into the gravel drive of the U-Haul parking lot, I contemplate how long I'll need this unit. Maybe I could rent some space in Liza's barn and just haul everything there until I save enough money for a house of my own.

Driving through the rows of containers, I head for the aisle in the back I know to be mine and park in front of the five-foot wide garage door. Except, when I put the car in park, I notice the lock is hanging loose from its hinge.

"What the hell!"

I glance down the line, noticing a few doors open with workers inside, but nothing out of the ordinary. Did someone break in?

Carefully, I climb out and inspect the picked lock, shoving it into my coat until I have time to buy a replacement. I lean my ear against the tin, eavesdropping to make sure no one is inside who could hurt me. Silence.

"Someone better not have stolen my crap," I mumble, lifting the heavy slide. It creaks and groans on the way up, but it's the sight inside that makes me cringe.

My boxes lay in shredded pieces on the floor. Some knifed. Some ripped and torn away from the tops until they're flayed like a butterfly. Dust floats through the beams of light, let in by the door, and I know whatever clothes I find are going to be a mess. So much for carefully vacuum sealing the fabrics before packing.

Frowning, I bend to ruffle through the closest box. Nothing inside seems to be damaged, just... dirty. Like someone broke in here to annoy me. Who the hell would do that?

The boxes stacked with books and my few mementos from my childhood aren't damaged at least. Maybe the person got interrupted.

Glancing down, I know I can't leave my stuff like this. I scoop an armload and haul it to my backseat. Ten more minutes and my back seat looks like the pigsty in my worst nightmare. Guess there's no doubt I need a shopping trip now.

It's still early in the day, so I text Liza to see if she wants to meet before we planned.

Liza: Sure thing! Would it be okay to bring Fiona until Smith's dad gets out of physical therapy?

Me: Absolutely! See you at one?

Liza: "The Black Olive?"

My stomach growls at the thought of pizza. *Hell's yeah!* I text her just that, happy to no longer be on that stupid wedding diet.

A fresh motivation takes over as I head to my new sanctuary. Thank god the place has a washing machine. A tiny washer-dryer combo unit, but it's better than going to the laundromat and wasting time.

To make things easier, I park in the alley, knowing it'll take multiple trips to carry the ripped boxes upstairs. Inside my apartment, I dump the first load into the wash, and get it started while I finish unpacking.

On my third trip down the stairs for, I spot Aaron by my car, putzing around the backseat.

"What the hell are you going here?" I move to the opposite side of the car from Aaron, needing the buffer to keep his toxicity from affecting my day.

"Why do you have to be like that?"

"What way? You're the one who broke us off, remember? You lost your right to ask me anything."

"I broke nothing. It was a little indiscretion, Melanie. Nothing to throw away four years on."

I scoff. "You threw it away. Not me." Straightening my shoulders, I nail him with what I hope is a *fuck you* stare. Since starting over on my own, I'm realizing how much I let people run over me in the past. "Besides, you said I wasn't worth your time, so why do you keep wasting it bothering me?"

He glances up at the worn stairs and the slightly dingy exterior. "I could get you out of this mess, you know. Give you everything you ever dreamed of." He backs away slowly toward Main Street, and I feel the tension in my chest lessening with every step. "I'm not giving up, Melanie. When you wise up, you'll be back."

"Keep dreaming, dumbass," I mumble, slamming—and locking—my car door.

A few hours later, by the time I leave to meet Liza, I've washed and folded two loads, and separated another for dry cleaning. I snatch my key off the hook and scan the alley before I walk down the stairs. Running into Aaron twice around my apartment makes me nervous about walking to the pizza place. Besides, if I find anything I like, I don't want to haul bags back on foot.

I luck into a spot on Main Street, right between Black Olive and a few of the boutique stores. Liza sits on the bench out front, scrolling through her phone with baby Fiona sleeping in her lap.

"Hey girlie," I whisper-yell to not wake the baby. A big ole smile lights her face as she locks Fiona into her laid back stroller seat before rushing to give me a hug. One hug eases some of the leftover stress from Aaron's visit.

"Ready for girls' day out?"

"Heck yeah. I need this more than that glass of wine we're having at lunch."

She chuckles and links her arm with mine, pushing the stroller one-handed like a veteran mom. "Let get our pizza on, then."

Inside, we pick a booth that we can park the sleeping baby beside and grab the tiny menu propped behind the salt and pepper shakers against the wall. While we wait for our server, I fill Liza in on Aaron's recent visits and her jaw hits the ground.

"What the hell? Please tell me you smacked him with a frying pan at least once."

To hide my snicker, I focus on unrolling my napkin and placing it on my lap. "Thankfully, no smacking... knowing Aaron's mom, she'd sue me for messing up his nose job she paid so much money for." I pause, wondering if opening this can of worms is a smart idea or not. "Well, uh... the first time Tyler was there and sort of tossed him against the wall when Aaron wouldn't leave."

"He what!" Our server bringing out waters and taking our drink order interrupts Liza's screech, thank god! Once the guy turns around, she's back at it. "Details. Tell me details. Did Tyler hit him? What did Aaron say about you being with Tyler? Wait... are you with Tyler?"

I bite my lip, debating on how much to say. "Tyler has been around. A little more than handyman service calls for." That's an understatement. There's not been a single day this week that he hasn't called or stopped by with a little surprise, or just for no reason other than to get a kiss. "It's like he's courting me, which is ass-backwards because we've already slept together."

"You slept together! Oh, my god! Oh, my gawd!" This time her screech draws eyes our way. Probably for the juicy sex life gossip. Great!

I slap her arm across the booth. "Stop it, would ya. I don't need to be the center of more gossip after the wedding debacle. Imagine what they're going to spread around town." My eyes fall to the menu in my hand as a distraction. "Maybe Tyler doesn't want news that he slept with me flying all over town."

Liza reaches across the table and squeezes my hand. "Of course he does, sweetheart. If he didn't, it would only be to protect your reputation. Tyler isn't a womanizer, Mel."

I nod. I know deep down Tyler isn't a womanizer. But thinking it versus his lifelong friend saying it are two different things. We let it drop when our drinks get delivered and decide to share a Caesar salad before our pizza. Once the waiter scoots away, the conversation turns to her end of month wedding and the tiny details she has left to plan.

"Anything I can help with?"

"Nah. Just bring your pretty self and get ready for some spa treatments and skiing. Do you think you and Ty will drive up together?"

I shrug. "I don't know… maybe."

Just then, the bells over the door jingle and Liza's face lights up. "Speak of the devil."

Tyler grins and walks over to our booth, his dirty work jeans and scratched up boots looking sexier than they should be. He's dusty, his hat turned backward over that sweaty flop of hair. Although, it looks like he changed shirt before coming inside.

When he gets close enough to slide a hip in our booth, he does, dropping a chaste kiss on my temple, before turning to Liza. Her shit-eating says it all, and I feel my face heat. "How are you fine ladies today?"

"We are lovely. Going shopping right after lunch," Liza says. "Maybe for a date dress..."

My face grows hotter and Tyler's grin aims my way. "Is that right?"

"Maybe." He grabs my thigh under the table, not buying my nonchalance.

Thankfully, he lets it go. "I should go wash up before my order's ready. Enjoy your afternoon." He stares right at me, making no effort to hide whatever this relationship is. "I will see you at seven. Okay?" That little hint of vulnerability right there keeps me from backing out. I believe Tyler is different than most guys. I'd be an idiot if I didn't give him a shot.

I nod, my tongue feeling too thick to answer without a squeaky voice.

With that, he's gone with a parting wave and a wink for me. When I turn back to Liza, she's trying her damnest to hide her laughter inside her napkin, but her shaking shoulders and eyes dancing with excitement give her away.

"Shut up." Laughing at myself, I take a sip of water and lean back in the seat, ready for an afternoon of gossip and girl talk I haven't had in ages.

Chapter Nineteen

Tyler

Melanie's shock when I kissed her in the restaurant plays on repeat in my head. It shouldn't be fun to turn Melanie's face red, but it is... especially now that I know the flush runs all over her body when she's embarrassed.

I've got two more jobs to finish before I can head home to get ready for our date. Ms. Betsy's hot water heater is almost done. I should have her hooked and ready to shower in an hour. I'm dying for one myself.

Inside, I drop the large pizza I brought on her table. "Lunch, Ms. B!"

Her padded feet shuffle into the kitchen. "I told you not to being me anything, you man. I'm just fine fixing myself a bologna sandwich."

"Nonsense. I was there for my lunch, anyway. Might as well share." I put on that dimpled grin my dad says gets me anything with the ladies.

She pinches my cheeks. "Don't you start with that, dear. I'll have a slice."

"Two." Shoving off the door, I leave her to enjoy her lunch. "I'm going to go finish up Ms. B." She grumbles something I can't hear as I enter the basement, but I know nothing good from delaying with that spunky little grandma.

Downstairs, I only need to finish the house connections and light the pilot. Knocking that out fast is easy. I check my watch, cringing that it's already 2:30. I make quick work of the hookups and pack my toolbox. I need to get to city hall before they leave for the day.

I make use of the utility sink in Betsy's basement to wash up my arms. I take my shirt off to splash my face and chest with the frigid water, hoping it freshens me up better than what I gave Melanie at lunch today. I cringe when I think about how sweaty and dirty I was sitting next to her today. God, I probably like a skunk run over and left for days.

I'll have to make it up to her tonight. I need to be on point.

Unfortunately, to do that, I can't get caught up in one of Betsy's long-winded stories. "Bye, Ms. B!" I call from her back door. "Everything is ready to go. Just let me know if you need anything else."

"Oh, yes. Thank you so much, Ty. Stop by for some fresh cookies next week. I've got a bachelorette party to prep for. You can be my tester."

I chuckle and walk out the back door, shaking my head. Looks like I'm going to be eating iced dicks next week. Betsy's naughty cookies are infamous during the wedding season.

Five minutes later, I pull into the nearly empty parking lot at town hall and gather the folder with my permit application and schematics of planned repairs. The cinderblock building doesn't look like much, with its cream exterior and bulky juniper planters flanking the door.

Inside, a blast of heat slaps me in the face. Normally, I'd welcome the warmth, but not after spending six hours sweating my ass off in Betsy's basement. Luckily, there's only two people waiting in line, so I take a number and take a seat, watching people come and go through the main door.

"Tyler." The little old lady working the counter looks ready to clock out for the day. Her eyes are listless, a frown creasing her lips down.

"This should be fun," I mumble, plastering on a smile before I walk to the open service window. "Morning, ma'am. I just wanted to check the status of my permit. It should have been dropped off yesterday."

"What's the address?" I rattle off the numbers I know by heart, watching her fingers fly across the keyboard. "Hmm... Let me pull up our notes." The longer she takes reading her screen, the higher my nerves spike. "I see what happened here." She pauses, clicking a few more buttons. "Yeah... looks like your permit was pulled by one of the higher ups. It's marked rejected."

Her blank face turns my way, as if that answer solves my dilemma instead of creating new ones.

"Why was it denied? Does it say?"

She shakes her head, scrolling the screen again. "It's signed by the CBO. That's all I see. You can call the main office and set an appointment."

Frustrated, I tap my knuckles against the counter. "Where's his office?"

She points to the staircase in the back. "Up and to the right." Snatching my folder, I head toward the back. "Mr. Jackson, you should call first. It's almost closing time."

I scoff. If they cancel my permit without so much as an explanation, they're going to get a surprised drop in. Taking the stairs two at a time, I wrap on the door that says Building Official. When there's no answer, I turn the handle and poke my head inside, aiming to figure out if the guy left for the day.

However, the picture waiting for me inside is the last thing I expected. Dressed in preppy polos and starched khakis, Aaron and the building inspector sit at his desk with matching paunches, looking every bit the fat cats they think they are.

"What the hell is this?" I ask, stepping into the room.

"This is my private office, young man." He stands, fists resting on the wood surface as Aaron smirks. He makes no move except to adjust the tacky gold watch on his wrist.

"I need a meeting to discuss permits." Aaron's face flashes with satisfaction, and my back stiffens. "What do you have to do with this? Why are you here, anyway? Didn't you move back home with mommy?"

His face falls, ears turning red as he stands, that puny chest puffing out as if he could finish any beef he starts. I chuckle at the sight and Mr. Eaves waves Aaron to sit. His reddened face is the best reward I could ask for, and I smile.

"Mr. Jackson, I don't have time for a meeting right now. If you talk to Mandy, she'll set you up for Monday."

"I need to fix this asap, sir."

"Nothing we can do about it today. Work will be here on Monday. Won't it, my boy?" He glances at Aaron with way too much familiarity for my taste. I squint at the side of his face, but the little punk won't even look at me.

Eaves packs up his briefcase, signaling the end of this discussion. Arguing in front of Aaron would mean admitting weakness, anyway. I'm not about to do that. Not when I have a sinking feeling that my permit issues stem from the cocky ass sitting there in that chair.

"That'll be fine, Mr. Eaves. I'll get on your books for first this Monday morning." I pause, noting the smug satisfaction on Aaron's face. There's no doubt he's up to something. "I have a hot date to get ready for, anyway."

Eaves chuckles, having no clue my last barb hits its mark. Aaron's fists tighten on his armchair. With that victory in my corner, I say my goodbyes and tap the door on my way out, already working plans in my head on how to work around this little ob-stacle.

For now, my sole focus belongs on the gorgeous female waiting for me to pick her up for a nice night out. Speaking of...

Me: You still got a table for two with my name on it?

A few minutes passes, which is understandable since Smith is in the middle of dinner prep, but by the time I'm back at my truck, a thumbs-up emoji confirms our evening will be everything I hoped for my date with Melanie.

Chapter Twenty

Melanie

Butterflies dance in my stomach as I check my reflection... for the fifth time.

Liza convinced me to wear it down and wild tonight, so after I showered, I diffused my frizzy curls with a smoothing oil and rubbed every inch of my skin with my favorite lotion. Excitement flushes my cheeks pink without using blush. Makeup is not my favorite thing, but two swipes of mascara frame my eyes perfectly without looking overly painted. A tinted Chapstick softens my lips and I grin, remembering Tyler's lips trailing all over my body. I may have a little extra padding, but Tyler doesn't seem to mind. And I'm tired of worrying about it.

The little black dress Liza convinced me to buy skims my curves perfectly. A satin ribbon ties just below my breast, putting those babies on a display shelf. Old Melanie—pre breakup Melanie—would cover myself with a cardigan.

New Melanie stares back at me from the mirror with slick waves and a smile I actually feel.

To top it off, I got a new client this afternoon at one of our shopping pit stops. Liza knew the owner and introduced me as someone who could take over her social media marketing and launch the new online boutique so the owner can expand her sales base. It's invigorating to see my life finally moving in a positive direction.

A loud knock interrupts my daydream, and I glance at the clock. Tyler is thirty minutes early, but at least he saved me from fretting in front of the mirror for the next half hour. I grab my heels and clutch and hurry for the door.

"Coming!" Puffing into my hand, I check my breath one last time and open the door. "Hi—"

My greeting cuts off at the sight of the empty landing. Where the hell is Tyler? The back alley is completely empty, except for my car. "Ooo-kay."

A long, rectangular box leans against the railing that I pick up before heading inside. The outside is matte white, no markings or logo at all, except for the crushed velvet bow holding the lid on.

I drop my shoes on the floor by the counter and untie the bow. Inside are the most beautiful, long-stemmed roses I've ever seen.

"Wow…" I lift the bundle and sniff. The flowery scent fills the kitchen and I smile. Roses have never been my favorite, but these are gorgeous. I'm not sure why Tyler sent me such an expensive bouquet when I'll see him in a few minutes, but I might as well have them in a pretty vase when he gets here.

Shifting them to the counter by the sink, I pull down a vase and snip the bottoms. I've just finished prepping the water when another knock sounds at the door. Quickly, I stuff the stems inside and set the arrangement on the table where Tyler can see before rushing for the door.

"Hey!" Tyler's dimpled smile hits me the moment I get the door open. *Gah! He's freaking gorgeous.*

"Hey, yourself." Leaning in, Tyler grabs the back of my head, under the thick curls, and lifts me for a kiss, just a teasing brush of his lips, but it sets my toes on fire, all the same. When he pulls away, I notice the wildflowers squished between our hug. He holds them out. "These are for you."

"Aww, you didn't have to bring me flowers. The bouquet you sent earlier was already too much." I reach up and wrap his neck in a hug, but when I pull away, a confused look replaces his smile.

"What flowers?" he asks, scanning the room. When his eyes fall on the roses, his lips thin. "I didn't send you those roses."

My mouth drops and I step back. "What do you mean? I assumed..." Tyler stalks to the table and digs. "There's no card. That's why I thought they were from you."

His back stiffens as he stares at the red petals, plucking one of them off a bud and rubbing it between his fingers.

"Hey!" I step closer, resting my hand on the firm line of his back. "Come on, help me get down another vase for my pretty flowers."

At first, I think he doesn't hear me. His gaze fixed on the dozen mystery roses, but then his eyes turn to me, dark as night. "These are from Aaron." It's not a question, just a grumpy stated fact.

I scoff. "No, they're not. That's ridiculous." I turn my back, feeling unsettled as I head to the cabinet of vases and stretch to reach another colorful container that's pushed behind others. The hairs on the back of my neck stick up and I shiver. My life has become a freaking soap opera. And I never wanted to live inside a soap opera. I hate drama.

Tyler comes up at my back and reaches over my head. "That one?" he asks, pointing to the bright yellow ceramic I want.

"Yes. Now let me put my beautiful flowers in some water and we can go." I smile at the colorful assortment, creating beauty out of chaos. "I love wildflowers," I say, burying my face in their petals.

Tyler waits at my side, his presence filling up the tiny space of my kitchen. "They're not fancy and expensive like those."

Peaking at him from the corner of my eye, I notice his eyes are still locked on the roses, taking a little wind out of my sail. I don't need gushing compliments, but a simple, *you look nice,* would work wonders to start a date on a good foot.

"Personally, I love wildflowers, no matter their cost. They're crazy and free." I drop my voice. "Like I wish I were." The pristine roses mock me from across the room. "Maybe those things are from Aaron. He always preferred perfection over genuine beauty."

Silently, I turn back to arranging my wildflowers, transferring the ribbon from their plastic wrapping to the vase. "There." I grab the bulbous bottom and carry the assortment to my coffee table. "You ready to go?" I ask, picking up the heels I planned to wear tonight.

After sliding them on, and grabbing my clutch again, I turn to face Tyler, wondering if we can get past this mood that's fallen over our evening. Earlier, I felt on top of the world. Now, I wish I planned a pajama night in, instead.

Tyler steps into my space, bending so we're eye level. "I'm sorry." He pinches my chin and lifts my lips for a kiss. "Can we start tonight over?"

I cross my arms, intending to make him suffer a little bit longer, but Tyler's puppy dog eyes get me every time. That and the nibbling bites he trails along my jaw. I tilt my head, giving him more room as his lips close in on my ear.

"You look beautiful," he says, combing his fingers through one of my curls. "I'm sorry. I was too distracted to say that earlier." He takes my arms, uncrossing them to hold hands between us, playfully swinging back and forth. "How bout if I take my beautiful date to dinner, already?"

Two-Fourteen is everything I expected. Romantic. Elegant but in that down home comfortable way.

Tyler reserved a booth in the dimly lit back corner by the wall of wine. Mason jar candles flicker in the center of the table, giving the illusion of privacy in the middle of the crowded restaurant.

"You really do look beautiful tonight," Tyler says, taking my hand across the table.

"Thank you." My cheeks heat as I glance at our connected hands, wishing our appetizers were here for a distraction. "So your uncle owns this place?"

Tyler smiles. "Yep. He opened it ten years ago after he discharged from the Army. He always loved feeding people. Same with Smith, but he lost his way for a while. Uncle Tuck giving him a shot in the kitchen gave him focus to get his life back on track, big time."

"Sounds like your uncle's a good guy."

"He is." Tyler strokes a thumb across my knuckles, lost in the freckles there. "I hope you don't mind, but I ordered the chef's special for us tonight. They'll bring courses out as Tucker prepares them. I thought it'd give us more time to relax and talk."

"Sure. I've never had a chef prepare a special menu before."

"Hopefully, you like it." Tyler hits me with that dimpled smile and I have little doubt that I'll enjoy dinner. Even just because I get to look at him.

Right then, a waiter brings us two appetizer plates with a single scallop on each, wrapped in bacon with a caramel-colored drizzle on top. He sets down a tiny fork and walks away without a word, leaving us to dine in peace.

Tyler waits for me to take a bite, grinning when I moan around the explosion of flavors in my mouth. "Holy cow..." I cover my mouth as I chew. "Oh my gawd, that's the best thing I've ever tasted."

Satisfied with my response, Tyler slices into his scallop, eating half in one bite. I lift an eyebrow and he shrugs. "What? It's good."

When the waiter takes our plates away and refills our water glasses, Tyler and I order a second glass of wine and sit back to wait for our next course.

"I'm sorry about earlier," he says, lacing his fingers together on the table. "I didn't mean to overreact over the flowers." He pauses, his eyes darting around the restaurant. "That guy has always gotten under my skin. Since we were in middle school together. He always acted better than the rest of us. Every time he got a new pair of shoes or a game system, we all wanted."

I pat his hand. "I get it. He did that to me constantly. Bragging on his family's money and connections. Telling me my furniture and clothes weren't good enough, that he'd buy me ones that were more appropriate to be his wife. It was awful!"

Tyler frowns as the waiter drops an oblong bowl of soup. "That's bullshit," he barks, startling our server.

I offer the kid a smile, hoping we don't come across as total nitwits in this nice restaurant. I mean, Tyler is the owner's nephew, so I doubt we'd get kicked out, but the last thing I want is more gossip.

"At least I'm away from that toxic mess. I'll toss the flowers when I get home tonight."

"No! You don't have to do that." He reaches over, covering my hand with his warmth. "You deserve all the beautiful flowers."

"Yeah, but I don't need reminders of Aaron." I pull my hand free and dig into my soup. "No more talking about that ass."

Tyler smiles as he tucks into his meal, too. Conversation stays on lighter topics after that. His projects and working at the store. My marketing growth and how working freelance online has more flexibility than a stuffy office. Every course of dinner is delicious and even Chef Tucker comes out to say hi and slap Tyler on the back in that avuncular way.

When he returns to the kitchen, a waiter delivers the most beautiful brown sugar crusted cheesecake to our table. From his tray, he produces a snifter of honey colored alcohol that he rotates around the glass, covering every inch before he strikes a fancy match and lights the liquid on fire. A round of ooh's and aah's sound around the room at the waiter's show. Once he deems the snifter ready, he tips a long stream of fire over our cheesecake, tossing sprinkles of sugar into the flame that light up like fireworks at our table.

My mouth hangs open at the delicious sight when he pulls away with a slight bow. "Oh my god. That looks amazing!" I exclaim, taking one of the offered spoons.

"Dig in, beautiful." Tyler's charm is in full swing as he holds a bite of crusted goodness out on his fork for me to taste. I debate a split second, before leaning forward and sliding the yummy dessert off his fork. Our eyes lock, simmering with a new heat.

Maybe it's the end of the night anticipation. Maybe the wine loosened my nerves. Whatever the cause, I scoop a spoonful of sweetness and hold it out for Tyler. He grins, taking a bigger drag off my spoon than he needs, letting his tongue dart out and clean his lips in that way that drives me insane with memories.

"Well, isn't this cozy?" sneers the last voice I want to hear.

My back stiffens as the bubble of lust pops between Tyler and I. His playfulness disappears as if it was never there. The laughter in his eyes replaced with venom, looking for a target. That target is my idiot ex who apparently has zero common sense.

"Go away, Aaron." I wish blowing him off would work. Unfortunately, the man only wants what he can't have. Our relationship is a testament to that childish behavior.

Of course, he doesn't listen. His hip rests against the back of my booth, effectively trapping me in the space. Tyler drops his fork, his spine going ramrod straight.

"I believe the lady said to go away. Do you need me to explain exactly what that means? I'm more than happy to show you." His fists tighten on the edge of the table and I reach over, covering his hand with mine in an attempt to keep the peace.

Aaron holds his hands up in mock surrender, his face twisted in sick pleasure to get a rise out of us. "I'm simply enjoying dinner with a colleague." He turns to wave at a pot-bellied gentleman across the room and Tyler's face goes molten.

"You did it, you sonofabitch."

Aaron smirks. "Did what? I only thought I'd come see if Melanie liked the flowers I sent. Just an apology for her having to deal with the wedding fall out."

"She's lucky to be rid of your conniving ass. And if you ever send her flowers again, I'll shove those roses so far down your throat, you'll be shitting thorns for weeks."

Eyes stare all the way across the room, their whispers growing as the men's voices rise. A server hovers a few tables away, ready to intervene. Tyler stands from the booth, increasing my panic that they are about to fight in the middle of the town's only fancy restaurant.

Aaron's face resembles a lobster as he tries to stand to full height—still inches below Tyler. His eyes pinch at the corner, his thin lips curled down in a frown, with arms crossed over his chest protectively. He has the nerve to glance at me for help before turning back to Tyler with his nose in the air. "You get no say in what she does. Melanie will be back when she's done slumming it."

"Hey!" I rush out of the booth, intending to step between the two, but Tyler's fist is faster. He nails Aaron in the jaw, knocking his weight to the side and right into me. My back falls into the booth and I grunt, shoving Aaron's weight off me.

Tyler rushes to help me stand up, lifting Aaron's weight off me with minimal effort. "I'm sorry. I'm sorry."

I knock Tyler's hands away and straighten my skirt that's ridden way too far up my thighs. My elbow aches from where it hit the wood, and I rub the spot, my eyes bouncing back and forth between the two arrogant men. I ignore Aaron's offered hand and he just lifts a brow, wiping the blood collecting at the corner of his fat lip. Tyler growls, glaring at Aaron.

Huffing, I lean in, grabbing my purse from the seat, which brings a satisfied smile to Aaron's face. "Shove off. I'm going home." Tyler reaches into his wallet, hurriedly pulling bills to cover our check. I duck past them both, aiming for the hostess to retrieve my coat. Nosy diners follow me across the room, their whispers quieting as I pass.

"Melanie!" Tyler's deep baritone is more on edge than I've ever heard it.

I ignore him and cross my arms, impatiently waiting for the girl to grab my coat. The raucous restaurant noise is back at full volume. No doubt discussing our scuffle. By morning, I guarantee we'll be page one gossip. That's the last thing I need when I'm trying to build a new business in this town.

Tyler's warmth crowds my back. "Melanie, slow down." I glare over my shoulder. "Aaron left. Let's sit back down and finish dessert."

"No." The hostess passes me my coat and I turn for the door before the tears burning the back of my eyes fall. Tyler tries unsuccessfully to help as I jerk my arms through the sleeves, breathing a sigh of relief once we're outside, away from prying eyes.

Tyler grabs my elbow, pulling me to a stop and I jerk away, annoyed by the soreness already bruising the skin there. "Look, I'm sorry for throwing a punch. That's not like me... that guy just... he gets under my skin."

For what it's worth, he looks remorseful, and it cools part of my anger. I nod. "I get it. I'd love to throw a punch at the idiot, too." I glance up at the sky and the sleet starting to pelt my face. The chill seeps into my bones and I shiver. Tyler steps forward, his hands rubbing my upper arms to warm me up. I take a step back, meeting his troubled eyes. "This whole thing, though, proves I shouldn't attempt any sort of relationship right now. My life is too big a mess."

"That's crazy. Don't let Aaron win. He knew exactly which buttons to push..."

"I'm sorry." I shake my head, annoyed by the pain twisting in my chest. The lost feeling makes little sense, but it's there and it freaking hurts. "I need to go home," I say, turning toward my little apartment. I need to put space between me and Tyler before I forget why this is such a bad idea.

"Wait!" He steps up at my side. "I'll drive you home. It's too cold for you to be out in this." I pause and he drops a kiss on the top of my head. "I promise I won't say another word. Just a ride."

Sadness sweeps through my body, but I nod, resigned that this will be the last time I'm this close to a man like Tyler.

Chapter Twenty-One

Tyler

"What's eating your craw?"

I glare at Smith, whose grin is completely out of place on his sweat-covered face. We're both paint-splattered, dirty with sawdust, but my buddy is somehow bright as sunshine while I feel like the dirt under the Devil's boot.

Smith shakes his head when I go back to painting instead of answering. "Gotta get this porch finished. That's all."

I'd been happy when my permit passed the week after that awful date. Once I showed up Monday morning in Eaves's office with my paperwork perfectly in order, T's crossed, I's dotted, he couldn't argue or postpone, no matter what asshole had a hand in his pocket.

"You know there was a point, not that long ago, when you had to help me pull my head out of my ass."

"Don't know what you mean."

Smith chuckles and shakes his head. "Fine. Fine. I'll leave you alone... for now."

Just as I'm about to argue, the screen door slams under my ladder, and I cringe as the feminine voices carry to where we're finishing up our work.

Carefully, I hook the paint can on my ladder and climb down with the dirty brush, Smith following right behind with a big smile for his woman. I wipe the sweat off my face with my shirt, avoiding the eyes of the one woman I can't get out of my head. It's been two weeks since we spoke and it's killing me.

"Hey, Ty. You guys almost done?" Liza asks sweetly.

"Yeah." I chance a glance at Melanie, who looks horribly uncomfortable, despite our friends' cheery demeanor. Baby Fiona reaches her chubby little arms for me to pick her up and I melt. "Fifi, Uncle Ty is dirty baby." She squeals and I can't help but laugh, settling the little thing on my hip.

Melanie smiles, before dropping her eyes to her shoes, but I catch the pinking of her cheeks and it gives me hope. She's not as unaffected by me as she seems.

"We were just finishing up last-minute details for our trip," Liza says, latching herself to Smith, despite his sweaty stink. She gazes up as if he hung the moon. "Melanie has to get her car into Axel's shop, though, before she can drive up."

"Yeah, it's having trouble starting on the really cold mornings. I don't trust it heading into the mountains."

"She can ride with me," I offer before I think better of it.

Smith smirks. "Makes sense. Axel's wait time is usually a few days on bigger jobs."

Melanie's face turns red as she stutters a denial. I grin around Fiona's fingers that have found their way into my mouth. Gently, I tug her little wrist and kiss the tips, catching Melanie's eyes. "No sense in both of us driving when I've got room."

"Yeah, we decided to check Dad out early and drive him up with and the baby tomorrow," Smith says, worry crinkling the corners of his eyes. His dad's deteriorating condition worries us all. Part of me thinks their hurry for the wedding is so he'll be more coherent for it.

Melanie bites her lip, seeming torn on how much to argue.

I pass the baby back to Liza and take a step back. "How bout if I clean up this mess and go shower and I'll meet you at the shop and give you a lift home?"

She narrows her eyes, but I back up, already nailing the tops back on our paint cans. Liza beams and wraps her arms around

Melanie's shoulders. "I'll feel so much better if you aren't driving alone up the mountain."

"What about Lennox?"

Liza shakes her head. "She can't come up until school lets out. She'll be rushed as it is."

I haul the paint cans to the back of my truck and stow the brushes in a jar of mineral spirits until I get home to clean them properly. At the cab, I wave at our little group, my eyes locking on Melanie's confused frown. "I'll see you in thirty, Mel. I'll call ahead and let Axel know you're coming."

The next morning, I pull in front of Melanie's apartment armed with two large coffees and Danishes from French Kiss. She's down before I even kill the engine, dragging a large suitcase and a dress bag behind her.

"Couldn't wait to get on the road, huh?"

"Thought I'd make it easier on you, so you didn't have to come upstairs?"

"Don't trust yourself with me in your space?" The telltale blush that creeps across her cheeks gives me hope, and I smile, taking her bags and securing them with mine in the crew cab of the truck. She wouldn't let me walk her upstairs yesterday either, but we have a long ride ahead of us. Melanie has to talk or we'll both go crazy.

I head for her side, but she's up in the truck before I can open her door. "Damn, woman," I mutter, moving back to the driver's side. I blast the heat as I pull out onto Main Street, taking a fortifying sip of my coffee. "So, what did Axel say about your car?"

Her shoulders slump. "It'll be a week, just like you guys said. Something about the carburetor and he needs to order a part. I didn't pay a lot of attention after he gave me the timeline. I just hope the fix doesn't blow my savings account."

I glance her way, keeping both hands on the wheel so I don't grab her hand for comfort. "Axel's a fair dude. If anything, he tends to under charge women, because he's afraid of ripping them off."

Melanie exhales, looking relieved as she takes a bite of her breakfast. "Thank you for these," she says, holding up her sweet treat.

I grin. "Anytime."

Silence takes over the cab as we both devour our Danishes. The spiced coffee is a perfect complement to the sweetness, shaking off the tiredness burning my eyes from two weeks of minimal sleep.

"So, how have you been these past two weeks?" I ask, drawing Melanie's attention from the passing scenery.

She looks wary. "Things are fine. I've been working on a few clients in town and creating a web presence for my new business."

"Nothing new from Aaron?" I keep my eyes on the highway leading us out of town, so she doesn't see the irritation I have just saying his name.

"No. I see him in town, but no more flowers or drop-ins."

I nod. "Good. That dude's trouble."

She chuckles, shaking her head. "The dude is a wuss, that's what he is. I told you; he only wants someone else's shiny toy. Besides, you're the one who threw punches, so who's trouble, after all?"

A snort slips out that I try to cover with a sip of coffee, but she laughs at me, anyway. This time I do reach for her hand, pulling it center for a squeeze. "I hate to tell ya, honey, but I'd do it again. In a heartbeat. That asshole doesn't deserve to breathe your air." Guilt twists in my stomach. "My only regret is that you got caught in the crossfire. I should have been more careful."

"What about your uncle? Wasn't he pissed?"

"Nah, he knows I don't start trouble for nothing. Besides, he's had his share of hotheaded days." She laughs, and it feels like a victory that she doesn't pull her hand away. I twine our fingers. "I'm not giving up, you know?"

"What do you mean?"

"Just that. I'm giving you time to process this, but I'm not giving up."

A sweet blush coats her cheeks with a ghost of a smile before she turns back to the window, and I focus on the road as we get to elevations that narrow and wind.

Thirty minutes later, we are on the final stretch of two-lane road before I will need both hands and four-wheel drive to concentrate. A podunk gas station looms ahead and I signal, carefully pulling in front of the unleaded pump.

"I'm going to gas up before we hit the mountain."

"Oh, thank god. That coffee is pressing my bladder, something fierce."

I chuckle. "You could have said something."

She blushes. "I'm fine. I'll grab some road snacks while I'm in there."

"Sounds good." We hop out, and I follow her sexy back, sashaying into the store as I slide my card into the pump. I guarantee she has no idea she does that, but damn if those hips aren't hypnotizing, even with a baggy sweatshirt covering most of it.

I zone out as the pump rolls higher, groaning at the final number when the nozzle clicks off. "Damn inflation," I grumble, screwing the gas cover on. Constant traffic pulls in and out of the parking lot, solidifying my choice to stop and refuel now. This must be the last stop before the resort.

Since Melanie is strolling the aisles still, I head into the store to empty my own tank, passing her with a kiss on the head on the way. "I'll be out in a few."

When I'm done, she has water, protein bars, Chex Mix, beef jerky, and a roll of donuts. I laugh and her face turns bright red. "I wasn't sure what you liked."

I can't help pulling her into a hug and reach for a bag of Cheetos to add to the mix.

She glances at her haul, then scans my body. My cock notices and jumps with excitement. "You probably don't eat any of this junk, do you?"

"You saying I'm hot?"

"Shut up. You know you're hot, cocky." She swats at my stomach, and I grunt playfully, grabbing at her junk food before she turns away, hiding her smile.

She piles our stash on the countertop, tossing her card at the cashier before I get my wallet out of my pocket. "I was going to pay for that." I frown, but there's too many people around us to make a scene.

"Well, I got there first, so hah. Besides, you're driving."

The cashier grins at us as he packs up the goods, and we head outside. "It's an hour until we get there, right?" she asks, holding the bag open for me to pick.

"Yep." I snatch the beef jerky first and she opens my water, propping it in the console. Checking my rear-view mirror, I make sure the coast is clear before pulling onto the road. A dark tinted car pulls out at the same time, not looking the least bit snow ready. That guy's going to have a big problem if he goes very far up the mountain.

Nearly an hour later, we are only a few miles from our destination on the GPS. My tires slip a few times, jangling my nerves, but I try not to let Melanie see. All my concentration focuses on staying in the grooves of snow and watching for oncoming cars. The view off the side of the mountain would be beautiful if I weren't terrified of sliding off it.

Melanie's hand grips the grab bar as my wheels spin one more time. "Everything oka—" she starts, but a deafening pop startles us both.

The wheel jerks in my hands, becoming a hundred-pound weight as I try to keep the truck straight in the snow. "Shit!" I let off the gas and lightly pump the brakes, fighting the pull of the truck as it comes to a stop on the curvy mountain road. "You okay?" I ask, putting the truck in park. Her pale face worries me, and I reach over, stroking the hair away from those panicked eyes. "We're okay. I'm going to go check the tires."

"Out there?" she squeaks.

I nod. "We only have a few more miles to go." The steep angle of the snow battering my windshield lights a fire under my butt to move faster. We need to get to the resort before we become sitting ducks on the side of the road. I turn on the hazards, praying that any driver coming is cautious enough to drive in this weather and not run us over.

Melanie tosses me the coat and gloves I discarded in the back seat and gives me her scarf to wrap around my face. I smile. "Be right back."

Frigid wind hits me the moment I open the door, and I check both ways. Not a car in sight. I walk around the truck until I find the problem. My front wheel is shredded. Shard pieces sticking out from a bank of snow. *That tire was fuckin' brand new.*

Moving to the bed, I release the hatch that hides my spare and take it and the jack equipment to the front of the truck. Melanie hops out to follow me. "Woman, get back in the car. It's freezing."

She waves me off, zipping up her puffy jacket, as if that's going to help. "I can at least help you carry stuff."

I toss the new tire in the snow, unraveling her scarf to wrap around her own face if she's out here. The material muffles her argument as I bend down in the snow and brace the jack, pumping the handle just enough. Before it lifts off the ground, I loosen the lug nuts, handing the pieces to Melanie to hold while I remove the trashed wheel. Hauling the thing to the back, I scan the blown area, an uneasy feeling falling over me at the smoothness of the tear.

Not wanting to frighten Melanie, I stow it to inspect later and head back to brace the new tire. On my knees, the snow seeps into my jeans, wetting and chilling. I didn't wear all-weather pants, assuming this drive would be easy and all indoors. My gloves are too bulky to screw on the nuts. I rip them off, passing them to Melanie as I rush to get us out of this cold faster.

My fingertips numb on the cold metal, shaking slightly, but I lean over, hiding that fact from Melanie. I'm using the wrench to tighten the last bolts when a crunch of ice and snow alerts a car coming, one too fancy for snowy roads.

"Back up." I urge Melanie, standing between her and the truck, just in case the guy slides into us. He speeds by, too fast for the snowy road, even if he had a truck equipped to take the incline.

"They didn't even stop," Melanie says frowning.

"I know. Let's get out of here."

Rushing forward, I open her door, ushering her in before wrapping up my wrench set and the jack and tossing them into the truck bed. Melanie blasts the heat inside the cab and I take a few minutes to thaw my hands and slow my heart rate.

We both sigh in relief when the truck successfully climbs again and this time it's Melanie who reaches over and presses her hand to my thigh. I smile, keeping my grip and ten and two.

"I think I'm ready for a drink."

"My god! Me too."

The first thing I'm going to do when we get there is drag Melanie to the bar for a shot. We may not be in college anymore, but my damn frazzled nerves need it.

Chapter Twenty-Two

Melanie

*L**iza: Meet in the restaurant downstairs at 7:30.***

I glance at the bedside clock. Two hours.

I send back a thumbs up and sprawl on the plush bedspread in my fluffy robe. This afternoon, once Tyler and I unloaded the truck and checked in, he dragged me to the old-world bar tucked into the back of the lobby and ordered two *Royal Fuck* shots. The bartender lifted an eyebrow at our disheveled appearance but poured the drinks when Tyler slapped two twenties on the bar top.

There's something charming about his dominance I can't stay away from. He doesn't use it to push down others... Except for Aaron and I don't exactly mind taking Aaron down a peg or two.

The problem is, that whiskey went right to my head. Maybe lunching on convenience store snacks didn't put enough food to soak up the alcohol, or I've become a super lightweight. An hour-long bubble bath eased the rest of my nerves from that mountain drive, but now the bed is calling to my soul to take a nap.

I spread my hair back on the pillow to air dry and close my eyes, sinking into the mattress.

Knock. Knock.

"Ugh…" I roll out of bed, wondering if I forgot something at the front desk. Padding across the carpet, I cinch my robe tighter, not wanting to flash a poor bellhop. Except, the handsome face on the other side of the door doesn't belong to a hotel employee. It's the face that's followed me into my dreams these past two weeks.

"Hi," I say, leaning against the door.

"Hi." His dimpled smile promises things I swore I didn't want again.

Still, I open the door wider. "Come in."

He steps inside, glancing at the view of the mountain outside my window. "Looks a lot prettier from this angle," he says, his rich laughter filling the room.

"No doubt."

The setting sun silhouettes Tyler's shape as he steps forward, freshly showered with an ironed button-down tucked into steel gray slacks. It's the dressiest I've seen him, and I'm torn because

I really love his shirtless blue jean style. "You look nice," I offer, fighting a blush he'd easily see without my makeup.

He grins. "So do you."

My cheeks burn. "Stop. I just stepped out of the bath."

He chuckles. "It's a good look."

I fight a smile and move to the mini fridge. "Want a drink?"

"Sure." He steps forward, crowding my back. "I just stopped by to make sure you were okay after our drive up." His hands rest on my shoulders and I hold my breath, waiting for the delicious feeling of his body pressing close.

When it doesn't come, I leave the mini bottles of alcohol on the countertop and turn under his arms, resting my hips against the wood. "I'm fine, Tyler. I'm not a weakling." I'm tired of feeling like I have no power. Like life just keeps happening to me.

I'm done with it.

Lifting my chin, I undo the tie of my robe, shrugging it off my shoulders with more confidence than I've ever shown in my life. Underneath is the sexiest balcony bra and matching lace thong I own. It boosts my breasts to another level, which helps when the padding in other areas makes me self-conscious.

Tyler's gaze burning across my exposed skin goes a long way to fix any issues I have with my body. It's worth the pretty penny at the lingerie store. The vulnerability of being nearly naked against his dress clothes is such an unbelievable turn on that I reach up to undo the top buttons at his neck.

"What are you doing, Melanie?" His gravely voice hits me low, ramping my courage that I'm doing the right thing. I'm tired of holding myself back from happiness, like there's some timetable for propriety.

"What does it look like, Tyler?" I undo another button, licking my lips at the tan skin exposed.

His Adam's apple bobs as his fingers brush across the wide lace at my hip. "Melanie, there's no going back."

I freeze. "What do you mean?" Is he turning me down?

Tyler growls, his rough hands gripping my hips and lifting, resting my bottom on the dresser top so he can step between my legs. His smile is gone. And though his eyes are as soft as the caress of his hands, the laughter has disappeared. The rough fabric of his pants rubs my inner thighs where he holds me close. I feel the steel rod he's hiding, and it eases some of my nerves.

He wants me, at least.

His eyes search mine, one large hand coming up to lace in my hair. "I told you I'd wait, Melanie. You should know that if I have you again, there's no going back. You're mine." His forehead falls to mine, our breaths mingling in the close space.

Maybe this is exactly what I wanted. Why I wore my sexiest underwear to get under his skin.

Either way, he's right. "No turning back," I say, holding my breath.

A brilliant smile lights his face. "We don't have long."

I wiggle against the front of his pants, locking my legs around his hips, when he lifts and moves us to the bed. He drops my back on the bed, but I bring him down with me. "Too many clothes."

We both attack his buttons until he's free and I stroke my hands over the contours of his chest, leaning forward to nibble one curved pec, then the other, while Tyler fights to free his arms. "Damn dress shirt!" He tosses the shirt to the side, and I laugh.

"It's going to wrinkle."

"They'll get over it." Gently, he shoves me back to the bed and buries his face in my balcony of cleavage. "So fuckin' sexy," he growls, leaving bite marks in his wake.

I hear the clank of his belt but can't concentrate on anything except the freaking torture of his mouth, going everywhere except where I want it. "More..." I press my chest into his mouth, moaning when he rips the cups down and captures a nipple. "Yes!" A flood soaks my panties and I tilt my hips, searching for friction as my hands grip his head, guiding it to my other needy peak. "Tyler... please."

He jerks back, and I scream at the loss. Until his large body covers mine and I realize he's lost the pants and boxers. "I wanted to go slow, but I promise next time." He strokes the long length of his cock against my wetness, both of us moaning at the slippery glide across my clit. "Tell me," he says, notching my entrance, but not pushing in. He glides again across my sensitive nub.

"Tyler!" My fingernails dig into his lower back, dying to bring his body close.

"Tell me you're mine." The head of his cock spreads me wide, stopping just an inch inside.

I gasp, clutching at anything in reach. "Yes! Tyler, yes! I'm yours, dammit—ahh!" My voice cracks as Tyler buries himself deep in one long stroke.

He falls to his elbows, one hand diving under my rear to angle me tight against his groin. An animalistic sound echoes that I don't realize came from me until Tyler's grip in my hair tightens, exposing my neck to his teeth.

"Shit!"

His hips speed up, making it impossible to drag air into my lungs around the pleasure.

"This is going to be fast, baby girl. I need to you come."

My nails rake down to his ass, gripping the tight muscle as his teeth latch onto my nipple and I scream, convulsing… flying. The suction of his lips softens, riding the rhythm of pleasure pulsing below as he strokes shallow thrusts. One. Two. By the third, his back stiffens as he swells, burying himself deep, as pulse after pulse coats my insides. The feeling stretches my orgasm on, and I curl myself around his body like a koala, panting.

My thighs burn where they wrap around his width, but I hold still, stroking the light sheen of sweat on his back as his length glides through the wetness we created, as if he can't bring himself to pull out.

"Wow." I chuckle as Tyler lifts to look at my face. He pushes my damp hair from my forehead, matching my grin with one of his on.

"I hope that's a good wow, because woman, being inside you near about killed me."

I laugh again, something I've never done after sex, but the fact that he could even ask that question proves he may be the one who kills me.

Bending up, I capture his lips in a kiss, realizing we jumped right across the make-out line in the rush to get naked. "That was definitely a great wow." I sniff. "But I think we need a shower before we go to that rehearsal dinner smelling like sex."

Tyler grins like a kid in a candy store. "What if I want to smell like you?" He tips his hips and I'm surprised to find him still partially hard inside me.

"Oh, my god." I slap his shoulder and Tyler pulls out, laughing. Immediately, I feel empty and hate it.

"Okay, I'll give you a shower, but I'm coming with." He slaps my rear and I squeal, hopping off the bed and hustling to the bathroom with Tyler's warmth running down my legs.

He spends the next thirty minutes washing and tasting me thoroughly before pinning my chest to the wall and entering me from behind. This time, our love-making is slow and sensuous, full of touches too meaningful for so early in a relationship. I don't let myself think or deny what I'm feeling. I let go, reveling in the firm hold of Tyler's arms as he wraps me up like I'm precious and strokes us both to heaven.

After, we get dressed again side by side. I let my hair air dry, embracing the wild curls and swipe on a touch of mascara and lip gloss as my only make up.

For some reason, I don't feel like faking perfection tonight. Maybe it's the way Tyler looks at me, but I want to be on his arm as the real me and show the world.

Chapter Twenty-Three

Melanie

Waking up in Tyler's arms is the closest thing I've ever felt to heaven.

My body is deliciously sore, every muscle strained after multiple rounds of what I can only call 'work out sex.' No one in my past prepared me for the acrobatics of not being able to keep our hands off each other.

Thank god, Liza and Smith only wanted a nice, sit-down dinner before their wedding. Smith was adamant that no one in our circle needed practice walking down an aisle and he wanted to spend the night celebrating his little family.

I roll over, pressing my head to Tyler's chest in a little celebration of my own. Soon, we will both get up and go our separate ways for the day, tending to our friends. But this morning, nothing short of an avalanche would get me out of this bed.

I'm debating on sacrificing the warmth of Tyler's body to go get us coffee when the room phone jingles rudely. Tyler startles and I kiss his chest, rolling over to grab the handset to keep from waking him further.

"Hello."

"Miss Gussow, we have a delivery for you at the front desk."

"Now?" I glance at the clock. "It's barely 7:30. Can't it wait?"

"I'm sorry, ma'am. The delivery man insisted."

"Fine. I'll be down in a few." I hang up, and Tyler drags me back to his side, tucking me into his big spoon. His face buries in my hair and I relax, circling his arms with my own.

"Who was that?" he asks, groggily.

"Front desk. They have a delivery for me."

He squeezes me with a moan. "Sleep."

I chuckle, patting his hand to free myself. He groans adorably and rolls to his back, the expensive sheet riding low on his waist and torturing me with the ridges of muscles I explored with my mouth last night.

"I'll grab us some coffee while I'm gone," I say, turning to take care of morning business in the bathroom. By the time my teeth are clean, and I've changed into something presentable for the public,

Tyler is softly snoring in the bed. I slip out with my key card and wallet, closing the door gently behind me.

When the elevator opens onto the main floor, I head straight for the front desk, my feet stalling when I see a giant bouquet of red roses. *Those aren't for me. This is just some weird coincidence.* Besides, that vase is double the size Aaron delivered to me and threaded with white Calle Lilies. It must be an arrangement for someone's wedding today.

"Sir…" The front desk attendant finishes typing into his computer before turning my way. "Gussow. You said you have a delivery for me."

He nods, a massive smile splitting his freckled face. "Sure do." He motions to the dreaded bouquet. "This gorgeous set arrived for you this morning."

I shake my head before he finishes the sentence. "No. Those aren't mine."

His smile dims a fraction as he reaches for the base, barely able to see me around the arrangement as he tries to slide them my way.

I nod harder, stepping away as if the buds are radioactive. The poor employee looks at me as if I've lost my head… or grown two of them. "Ma'am, these are yours. You need to take them. We can't return to sender."

"Uh-uhn. Not happening. Donate them or something. I'm not taking them."

With that, I flip on my heel and head for the sanctuary of my room upstairs. Except, a shape in the corner grabs my eye and I stop. He's buried behind the morning paper, but I'd recognize those obnoxious dress socks anywhere. Aaron's favorites have tiny dollar bills all over them. I do an about face and stomp toward the side table the coward's hiding at.

"What are you doing here?"

The paper jerks down and I'm hit with Aaron's smug grin. "It's a free country, Melanie. I thought I'd like a snowy vacation. You know, get away for a few days."

"Bull shit." I don't care if the whole restaurant stares this time. I raise my arm and point for the door. "Leave."

"No." He slams the paper on the table and stands up, stumbling closer. Scotch wafts from every pore, and for the first time, I notice how disheveled he looks. His jacket is misbuttoned, the knot of his tie hanging crooked. The red in the fabric brings out the bloodshot streaks in his eyes.

"Actually, never mind. Go sleep off whatever stupor you drowned yourself in last night." I turn on my heel, but Aaron grabs my arm, jerking me close to his stink. I hold my breath and yank my arm free. "Aaron seriously. Don't touch me."

Guilt swirls as he falls back in his chair, looking like a kicked puppy. He brought this on himself. I have to remind myself of that the entire walk to the elevator. I tap the up button. "Hurry. Hurry. Hurry." My foot taps the floor, but I force myself not to turn around.

When the door open and I climb on, I release the breath I'd been holding and press the fifth floor. I don't know how I'm going to explain returning empty-handed, but I couldn't be in that lobby one more minute.

Now, I need to figure out how to keep Tyler and Aaron away from each other all day. Especially if Aaron is strutting around here drunk and buying more flowers. Tyler would shit a brick if he knew Aaron was still after me.

Gah! Why won't that guy give up?

Two hours later, after a shower blowjob distracted Tyler from his missing coffee, I stand in Liza's bridal suite, my hair up in fat foam rollers, and champagne in hand.

Lennox is working a curling iron across Liza's head, adjusting pins and clips into a very elegant waterfall of curls.

"You, my lady, need a refill," I say, collecting both women's glasses and carrying them to the ice bar set up in the corner. The champagne has gone down way too easy this morning, so I add a bit more juice to mine to slow down the fuzzy bubbles taking over my head. I carry the glasses back to my friends and take a seat, loving the comfy sweat pants set Liza bought for her bridal party. Ours are hot pink with bridesmaids glittered across the back. Liza's are white with Bride decorating hers.

"Are you hungry? Can I get you something to nibble?"

"She's ready to nibble Smith," Lennox says with a hiccup. "Damn, I better lay off the champagne."

Liza giggles. "Nonsense." Her hand falls to her stomach, and she shakes her head. "I'll eat soon. Right now, my tummy is having a field day with my nerves."

"Aww..." I reach over and squeeze Liza's hand. "You and Smith are amazing together. This is just the next natural step. And it's just us. None of us are going to care if you walk down the aisle with toilet paper on your shoe, or if Smith forgets his vows."

"Hey!" She slaps my arm, laughing. "Don't jinx us."

I chuckle. "I'm kidding. Your wedding is going to be beautiful, but the most important part is you and Smith walking out of there together."

"And Fi," she adds. "We're working her adoption signing into the ceremony, since we've passed the sixty-day waiting period for her mother to change her mind on terminating rights."

My eyes well up and I dab at the corner, having already done my foundation while Liza was getting dressed and kicking Smith out of the room. "You're going to be an amazing mom to that little girl."

"Stop it, you two." Lennox fans Liza's eyes, laughing. "I know we haven't finished make up but I don't want to have to start over."

I grin and settle back on the couch, waiting my turn with the hair guru. "What to you think the boys are doing today?"

"Scratching and farting, if I know those three."

Liza squeezes Lennox's hand. "I'm so glad Nash could come."

Lennox pulls back and eyes her incredulously. "Because of his farts?"

We all crack up, joking about the boys and their shenanigans. Lennox and Liza fill me in on a ton of stories Tyler would hate if I knew... I think.

By the time we've finished hair and makeup, and snacked on finger foods that wouldn't make a mess of our pretty outfits, I think I've fallen a little bit in love with Tyler. Learning his history from his best-friends feels a little like an invasion of privacy, but every antidote shared points to an extremely caring, protective man. He'd do anything for his crew, and he's proven that to them all over the years. They don't share anything from his military days, telling me those are his wounds to share, but I don't take offense. These two women love him as one of their own.

"Thank you, ladies, for inviting me into your circle." I wrap both in a hug, fighting another round of tears. Even Lennox sniffles, which makes me laugh, and I push away, holding Liza at arm's length. "Now, let's get you in your dress."

She squeals, hopping up and down. "Oh, my god! It's time, isn't it?"

Liza's dress is simple lace over a fitted sheath. There's no tulle or trains to connect, so there's not a lot to help without outside of her zipper. "Smith is going to have a fit when he sees you in that dress." The sexy cut contours perfectly to Liza's assets while somehow looking demure.

All of us ladies finish dressing at the same time. Lennox and I chose our own dresses in matching deep plum. My A-line halter cuts below the breast, accentuating my best features and minimizing my worst. Lennox exudes class with her slouched off the shoulder number, curving to fit her body and stopping an inch above the knee. With minutes to spare, we slide on our shoes and Lennox goes to the bar to pour another glass of champagne. "How about a toast?"

"I won't say no to that," Liza says, happiness beaming from her eyes. "To loyal friends," she starts.

"To crazy friends," Lennox adds.

"And to the men who put up with us." I lift my glass with a grin and we all clink, drinking the cool liquid before we head out the door.

The hallway is empty, reminding me for the first time today about my earlier run in with Aaron. I hope for all of our sake he's stayed away from the boys, or cut his ties and gone home completely. Honestly, I have no idea why he's bothering with this whole cat-and-mouse game, but there's too much future in front of me to let a dark cloud fall over it today.

Lennox, Liza, and I make our way to the venue hall at the back of the resort. Smith's dad and the wedding coordinator meet us there with excited smiles.

"Is everyone ready?" the coordinator asks. She's dropped into the bridal suite multiple times today, so she has very little doubt about the bride's eagerness to walk down the aisle.

Still, Liza takes a deep breath, and it whooshes past her lips. "It's finally time."

Mr. Blackburn steps carefully forward, using his cane for extra balance. He places a light kiss on the side of Liza's head. "Thank you for bringing my son back to me. And for that smile, he can't hide from anyone anymore."

Tears well in all our eyes.

"Thank you for walking me down the aisle, Dad" Smith's dad beams at the endearment, but it's Liza's watery smile that does me in and I dot the corner of my eye, avoiding running my mascara before walking down the aisle.

We line up in order of entry, and the coordinator signals for the French doors to open. Piano instrumentals welcome us into the flowery fairy world. Bougainvillea climb trellises arched over the door, flowing naturally with large leaf greenery in brilliant greens, yellows, and reds. Floor to ceiling windows flank the back wall, creating a wedding-centric greenhouse with a beautiful view of the mountains in the backdrop.

Clutching a bouquet of tulips and lilies in front of me, I begin the padded walk down the aisle, praying I don't trip on my heels. Smith, holding his daughter, makes an adorable picture, shifting impatiently as he waits for his bride. I hear Lennox begin her walk behind me as I'm halfway down the aisle, but the moment my eyes fall on Tyler in his dress blues, I can't look anywhere else.

The uniform cups his muscular thighs like a glove. His jacket fitted to those strong shoulders and V-shaped torso. Medals hang from both men's jackets, reminding me of their sacrifice, even without knowing the whole story. Each ribbon tells a story I can't wait to learn.

Tyler's eyes bore into mine as Lennox and I take our places at the altar. Even after the bridal march begins and all eyes turn to Liza, Tyler holds mine. Smith passing him Fiona so he could accept Liza's hands from his dad with a heart-felt man-hug, is the only thing to tear him away. My heart swells. Tyler is a natural with that little girl. She nuzzles her head into his shoulder, curling arms around his neck like she needs a nap.

There are few chairs in the room, being that this is just a family wedding and celebration, so we all mostly circle around the minister and couple, witnessing them professing never-ending love in personal vows. Tears stream down every face, even a few of the men, when Liza signs papers to adopt Fiona and hugs her tight between her and Smith as they share their first kiss as husband and wife.

Cheers and hugs converge on the couple until Fiona cries, telling us all to back out of her space. Liza is all smiles, though, gazing at her family with such love. Tyler finds me in the melee, wrapping his arms around my waist and hugging tight.

"You are so beautiful in that dress." He strokes the bare skin of my shoulder, swaying at my back in a sensual dance while congratulations get passed around.

"Who's ready for some good grub?" Smith asks, tucking his family into his side like they're his gold medal prize.

"Yes!" A chorus of cheers sound and we all follow the wedding party, chattering over the gorgeous room, the baby, and the new family's future plans.

Chapter Twenty-Four

Tyler

"I don't think I've ever, in my entire life, seen Smith this happy."

Melanie chuckles, low and sexy, at my side. My lips find the tiny freckles dusting Melanie's shoulder. "Have I mentioned, I'm pretty damn happy, too." I bite the soft skin there. "Especially with this dress."

"Stop..."

Her pointy little elbow nudges my ribs and I laugh, glancing around the table at our friends, heads tilted in their private worlds, laughing, snuggling. Our dinner was delicious, but now that it's done, I'm more than ready to get my lady alone.

"Wanna dance?" I ask against her ear, breathing in that delicious fruity scent that is so Melanie. My mouth waters. "Or maybe we bow out and head upstairs."

Melanie's laugh is music to my ears. "Let's dance."

I pull out Melanie's chair. "Congratulations to the happy couple, but I'm going to waltz my woman around the dance floor."

Smith grins and grabs Liza by the hand and stands. "I think we'll join you."

The four of us make our way to the dance floor by the sultry jazz singer, mingling between the couples swaying to her soulful rendition of a Sinatra ballad. I leave some space between us and our friends to give us all some privacy in the middle of the crowded dining room.

Melanie's arms glide around my neck as I pull her flush to my front, her curves molded perfectly against my impatient cock. She fiddles with one of my medals. "Have I told you how sexy you are in uniform?"

"Mmmm…" I spread my hands across her lower back, giving her a discreet preview of my appreciation. She flushes and I bend down, taking a nibble of her ear as we sway closer to the edge of the dance floor. "What if I sweep you out of here, *Officer and a Gentleman* style?"

She hums and tucks into my chest with a smile and closes her eyes.

Everything is right in the world.

My best friend is home and doing well with his new wife and daughter.

Melanie finally gave us a chance and is in my arms.

We rock back and forth for another four songs, ignoring the formal couples looping circles around us. Finally, the ensemble on stage calls for a break and a speaker pops to life with big band music.

Most of the floor clears, but I keep my hands on Melanie's hips, not wanting to leave our bubble, yet. She watches everyone make their way to the tables and suddenly stiffens.

"You okay?"

"Uh... yeah..." She pulls away, brows furrowed as she looks toward the back of the room. "I need to hit the restroom," she says, forcing a smile.

I lean down. "You sure you're okay? Do you feel sick?"

"No, no. I'm okay." She tips up and presses a kiss to my cheek. "I just need a minute. I'll meet you at the table."

"If you're sure," I hedge. "I'll grab us a drink" Melanie nods distracted, but I'm stopped from following her by Smith. His fat hand slaps my back, tugging me along toward the bar.

"I'm a married man, Ty. Can you believe it?" Roughly, he shakes my shoulders, jarring me on my feet.

I laugh. "Dude, never thought I'd see the day."

He shakes his head, but there's nothing but happiness bouncing off my friend.

"Two Macallan, neat. And a cabernet." He looks at me.

"Pinot Grigio."

The bartender nods and reaches for glasses to pour our drinks. I pull out my wallet. "I got it, man." I place my card on the counter for the guy to run and turn to Smith. "For real, though, I am so freaking happy for you and Liza. You both deserve all the happiness... Finally!"

He looks down at his fresh, titanium wedding band, a smile softening his tan face that I never used to see.

Our scotch glasses are set in front of us and we clink, taking a sip while the guy sets our respective women's wine down. Smith waits while the guy runs my card and I sign with a hefty tip. He grins at Liza all the way back to the table and I shake my head.

"You got it bad..." I snicker, and Smith smacks the back of my head.

Lennox and Nash have dug into a second piece of wedding cake, while Mr. Blackburn fawns all over his new granddaughter. Her little head lolls into the crook of his arms.

"I should get this one to bed," He says, moving to stand.

Smith starts. "N-no, Dad. We'll help you take her upstairs."

"I got it." Lennox stands, pulling Nash's hand. She smiles at Smith's dad, so the man doesn't feel insult over needing help. "No way can I let this little booger go to sleep without Auntie kisses."

Mr. Blackburn smiles softly, nodding as she takes the girl from his arms and he grabs his walking cane. "We'll get settled in the adjoining suite, son. I can handle tonight, so don't go worrying. You kids, enjoy yourselves." His earnest expression seemed almost pleading, and I felt horrible for both men. My friend didn't want to overwhelm his ailing father, but his dad wasn't ready to be put out to pasture, either.

"Thanks a bunch, Dad. Just knock if you need us."

"No worries. Now, come on, young lady, help an old man to bed."

Lennox startles, making the whole table laugh. "If that sentence came from Nash over there, I'd expect a lot of handsy grabby to happen upstairs."

Nash straightens. "Hey... I'm not old."

Mr. Blackburn pats her shoulder. "No worries from me, little one. But if you need tips for keeping your old man in line, I'll gladly share the goods." He winks at Nash, whose mouth falls open and Smith chuckles.

"Dude, I think your dad roasted me." He looks around the table. "I'm not old."

Laughter sounds around the table and Liza leans into Smith's shoulder with a sigh. I realize, looking around the table, that Melanie still isn't back from the restroom. I hope she's okay.

"Excuse me, guys."

Sitting my glass down, I scoot back my chair and head for the main hallway and the closest facilities. I hope Melanie isn't sick, but it's worrying me how long she's been gone.

Who am I kidding? The one-eighty she did on the dance floor worries me more.

My feet hit the floor with a mind of their own, all relaxation forgotten. The tables blend into the background where I dodge lingering dinner guests. Thank heaven I shed my coat when Smith and I returned with drinks. Melanie's glass of wine much be room temperature by now.

Turning left toward the restrooms, my heart rate picks up, giving me that same sense of dread that kept me out of harm's way that awful day Smith and half of our platoon suffered a disastrous IED. I remained with the half doing recognizance until I heard rumors of an ambush and got there just in time to triage minimum people. The day still haunts me. That I didn't know if time. That I couldn't do more.

My legs pick up speed, running now across the horrific floral carpeting.

Before the last turn, I pick up the panicked pitch in Melanie's voice. "What the hell do you mean?"

I freeze.

"You're not stupid. It works out for us all." My entire body freezes. Aaron.

"You're crazy."

A maniacal laugh sends chills down my spine.

"Not crazy. Pragmatic. Persistent. Whatever the fuck you want to call it? You made a hasty decision calling off the wedding."

A choked gasp from Melanie presses my head close to the wall, tipping around the corner just far enough to get an eye on the argument. Tears streak down Melanie's face where her back presses against the wall. My fists clench.

"*Mother Fucker*," I whisper, crouching low.

His voice slurs. *Shit.* "It was one little indiscretion, Melly. Once or twice. What's the big fuckin' deal? I was giving you the wedding." He stumbles and Melanie jumps, inching another step out of his reach. "You said yes and you and me were going to marry.

Then you go and fuck it all up!" Aaron's voice spikes at the end, his palm lashing out and slapping the wall by Melanie's head.

Murder grinds inside my head as I crest the corner, rolling my dress shoes to silence their heels. Melanie's hands shake, gripping the wall where Aaron leans over her. His fingers grip her chin, jerking her head to look at him. I bite back a grown.

Ten more steps.

"You're going to make this right, Melanie."

"Wh-what do you mean?"

"Dump the bumpkin, Melly. I'll give you ten minutes, or I'll come and find you."

"Aaron, we're over." Her voice catches. "Move on to-to some-one else."

"No! You will marry me. Soon." He jerks off the wall, pacing a few steps away, and I hurry forward. Melanie catches sight of me and gasps, her eyes widening in shock and a bit of relief. "My grandmother, the old bat, put in her will that I must be married at the time of her death to receive my birthright... my inheritance."

Melanie's jaw drops. Five steps.

As Aaron turns, eyes wild inside his mottled face. I lurch, closing the space with an arm extended, taking Aaron to the floor with my arm locked around his waist. The air rushes out of his lungs and

I'm up, kneeling over his prone form. I can't stop myself. My fist lands against his jaw, shooting fire through my knuckles.

Melanie's scream stops the hit from becoming twenty. "Tyler!"

I flip Aaron on his back, jerking one wrist as high as I can between his shoulder blades, my knee compressing his lower spine. "Go get Smith."

Those delicate feet start to step closer, but Aaron twists, squealing when my hold on his arm smarts and Melanie takes off.

"I'd shut up if I were you, jackass."

"Get the fuck off me, asshole. Do you know who I am?"

I laugh, the sound harsh to my ears.

"I'll ruin you for this," he says, drawing me away from the approaching footsteps. "She's mine." He tries to wiggle from my grasp, but I just laugh, silently thanking my father for the supreme patience to not tear this scum limb from limb.

The pound of boots and heels muffled on the hallway carpet. A carpet I grind Aaron's cheek into just as a shout from a security guard dents the haze of fury muffling my friends' voices.

"That man attacked me," I hear Melanie explain, when the security guard tries unsuccessfully to pull me off Aaron. We both end up jerked from the floor, the balding employee completely inept to handle someone even Aaron's size.

"Would you like to press charges, ma'am?"

Liza wraps her arms around Melanie's shoulders. "Damn right, she does."

"Ma'am?"

"Melanie, tell them who I am." Whisky wafts off the man, filling the hallway with the nauseating smell of sweat and unwashed clothes. Indecision and doubt war under her narrowed eyes. "Melly! I can fix everything. Just come home with me."

Her jaw locks, and a sense of dread falls over me as she steps closer. Aaron's smarmy smile scans down her body and he jerks his arm. I let go under the guard's watchful stare. Smith angles in front of Liza, ready to step in as backup at the first signal.

To my annoyance, Melanie steps into Aaron's personal space, angling her face up with a snarky smirk. "Officer, this is my ex," she says, locking his eyes with no fear. "He's been stalking me. Harassing me." She smiles sweetly, pointing at the wall right behind our head. "He trapped me here and took a swing."

"Fuck you!" He lunges and all three of us men move in at the same time.

I lock Aaron's elbows behind his back. Smith's arms circle Melanie and tugs her behind him with his new bride. And thank god, the unassuming security for the hotel steps between us all, his TASER out and narrowed on Aaron.

"Hands up, son." Aaron is smart enough to listen, his good sense seeming to weigh with his loss of control over this situation. The security guard looks as if this is the most exciting event of his year, his eyes bright, hands slightly shaking on his radio. "You've taken the choice away from your lady here."

I growl at Melanie being called his lady. *Bullshit.*

He clicks the transmit button. "Earl, ring PD, would ya? We got a disturbance here. Going to need the drunk tank at minimum. Possible 133."

She puffs out a breath, meeting my eyes around Smith's shoulder with a finality in her eyes. I cock my head and she smiles, easing the iron lung squeezing in my chest.

Earl calls back through the radio. "You need backup, Ray?"

Ray scans my uniform and Smith's, eyeing the muscles in his arms visible with his jacket removed. He puts the radio to his lips. "Nah, we got it covered."

Respect shines in his eyes as he nudges his head toward the front lobby, and I turn Aaron with more strength than is necessary, digging my fingers into the soft flesh of his inner elbow. The man stumbles and Smith chuckles at my back, leading the girls in our wake.

"Text Nash and Len," he says, and Liza nods, pulling her phone from some hidden pouch in her dress. I do a double and she grins.

Aaron's feet drag. "Keep moving, asshole."

Our next few hours are spent filling out police reports and taking statements. I stay by Melanie's side, refusing her an inch of space. I refill her water, hold her hand, rub her back, and at the end of the night, I drive us back to the hotel where we crash from exhaustion and sleep for the next thirteen hours before we're able to shake off the drama from the night before and enjoy the rest of our friends' wedding weekend.

Chapter Twenty-Five

Melanie

It's been months since Liza and Smith's wedding, and this is the first Saturday I've been free to do whatever I want.

Today, I ignore all the guilt that says work on my new clients' accounts. I haven't knocked out groceries or my meal prep for the week.

Normally, Tyler works Saturday mornings at his dad's store unless a client calls with an emergency. He's still working on a few things at Liza's farmhouse, but generally, by dinnertime, he's here with me, having dinner at home and alternating movie choices, or he's taking me somewhere new around town. Whether it's one of *The Most Romantic Town in the South* items, like the lock wall or one of the lovey-dovey festivals, or some of the other bucket list items we've been checking off for one another.

Tyler has traveled a lot more—and seen a lot more—in his life-time, so the things I plan for him usually involve pampering and relaxing. I like taking care of him, because my god, the man will do anything in his power to make me smile. Let alone all the giving he does around the community.

Dropping on the couch, I snatch the remote and prop up with my favorite pillow, legs curled under me. It's too warm now for a blanket, but the super buttered popcorn in my lap is exactly what I need to feel pampered today. Well, my favorite snack and some trash t.v.

Usually Tyler and I watch cooking shows together, and he'll even watch some of the *Survivor*-esk reality shows. But when I do my chores on the weekend, I indulge in all my *Bachelor* and *Love Island* shows. If I asked, Tyler would watch with me, I know.

Aaron never would.

I press play and watch the recap for last week's elimination, but before the show gets through credits, the key turns in my front door. Tyler is the only person other than Kitty with a spare key. I gave it to him the weekend after the wedding.

Shockingly, I actually feel safer knowing he can come and go. Trusting him with my safety and my apartment's safety is a no-brainer.

"Hey, babe!"

"Hey! Wanna watch some trash?"

Tyler's smile grows, warming his soulful eyes as he takes in my disheveled appearance. My hair sticks out from my head where I loosely tied a top knot. Baggy gauchos hang off my hips, paired with a tank top, no bra.

"This is your plans for this special birthday?"

"What's so special about twenty-seven?"

"Another year of the most beautiful woman on the planet." He bends over the couch, straightening and then straddling my thighs. I smack his chest, but that smile is worth being cheesy.

"Stop it. We have dinner later. I figured today, I'd just veg."

"Veg?"

"Yeah. Crap t.v. Crap clothes."

Tyler leans forward and bites my collar bone exposed by the spaghetti straps. "I approved the clothing. Easier to remove." His lips trail down to the curve of flesh pressed over my tank. When he stays on top of the cloth, sucking my nipple with a soggy buffer between the mouth, I want all over me. He stops, dropping his forehead to my breastbone. The moan against my skin makes me giggle.

"What's wrong?"

"We've got bucket list plans today, and right now I want to do nothing more than lay right here and get you naked. Maybe deliver some birthday spankings."

I wiggle underneath him and glance at the clock over the television. "Plenty of time before dinner..."

He grins. "Delaying the inevitable." A bandana appears from his back pocket, perfectly folded and clean. Not his usual sweat rag from a day of work. A question lingers in his gaze as he holds it in front of her eyes, silently asking the question. At my nod, he wraps the cloth around my eyes and I gasp, reaching up to touch the darkness. "Damn! That's hot."

I feel myself blush under the maroon paisley cloth, laughter flitting between us. "Should I change clothes?"

"You don't need clothes."

With that cryptic answer, Tyler curls my arms around his neck and lifts, kneading the thickness of my ass in his massive hands as my legs grab his waist. I can't see a thing, but I feel him make his way for the door, and other than a stupid amount of embarrassment for anyone who may see me hanging off this hulk-like dream.

Sunlight bleeds through my mask, my body bouncing against his hard stomach, sending a rush of excitement as he carries me down the stairs outside. "You better not drop me."

His chuckle is everything, and suddenly whatever crazy plan he has for my birthday, I'm game for.

Thick musk permeates the air, and I grimace, dislodging my eye covering slightly.

"I know. I know," Tyler says, his chest shaking against my back. "Ignore the smell for now."

I chuckle, my feet stumbling as Tyler guides my shoulders forward. "Are we there yet?"

"Yes, Miss Impatient." He turns my body in a circle quickly.

"Hey!" Two twirling rotations later, Tyler stops me suddenly, wrapping his arms around my waist. His warm breath tickles my ear where his chin rests. He kisses the side of my head and then my eyesight is back. The sunshine blinds me momentarily where it streams through the canopy of trees overhead. "What's this?"

His craggy, masculine laughter breaks up the silence of the secluded thicket. "What does it look like?"

I step out of his arms, the splash of steaming water calling to me. "It's beautiful." I reach into the stream of water cresting over the jagged rocks. The narrow cascade tinkles into a large, bubbling pool at my feet.

Tyler steps up at my side, his woodsy scent overtaking the less than awesome scent of the springs. "I promised I'd bring you here. We just needed some warm weather."

"We don't have our swimsuits."

A mischievous grin lights his perpetually tan face. My brain trudges, as if marching a hamster wheel and getting nowhere. One brow lifts and it dawns on me. "Oh..." He laughs, reaching out to stroke my flaming cheek.

"Well, we've marked a few bucket list items these past few months. Seems a mighty big shame that my woman has never been skinning dipping."

A little zing flashes through my chest like it does every time he calls me 'his woman', but... "I also have never been arrested. And I don't want to change that today either."

"Aww... that could be kinda fun on your birthday. It'd be a day to remember."

I glance over. "No."

"No fun." He pouts before stepping back, working the buttons on the front of his shirt from the bottom. Each disc slipping free offers a tantalizing peek at the taut skin below. I lick my lips and Tyler grins, nodding his head to me when his shirt is finally free.

One more glance at the steaming water does me in. Not a soul is around. What could it hurt?

Unlike Tyler, I'm not brave enough to strip slowly. Especially not in the open woods. Tyler's shorts pool at his ankles, sending a rush of excitement that strips my clothes faster than I ever have in my life. My hands shake as I rip off my shirt, but the light in Tyler's eyes urges me on. I toe off my shoes and rip my bottoms off, underwear and all, tossing them away from the water. The air freezes in my lungs as Tyler steps past me and launches himself, fully nude, into the water.

"Ahh!" My shock echoes off the forest as a cannon of water splashes my feet. Quickly, I rid the bra, adding it to my pile before gathering enough confidence to leap after Tyler, who's following my every move.

When my head pops up, his gorgeous smile has me floating closer. I'm a sucker for those dimples, and while my feet don't touch the ground at this spot, Tyler looks as steady as the stone around us.

He reaches out, grasping my waist to bring my wet nakedness against his front. "Mmm... happy birthday to me," I say, wiggling my legs to wrap his waist. The movement brings our eyes level, my arms circling those strong shoulders to hold myself upright. My nails scratch the buzzes hair at his nape, sliding up to massage the longer strands falling loose at his ears.

With my weight in one hand, Tyler backs to a rock formation at the edge of the spring and sits, pressing my lower back to keep our bodies locked close. The smattering of course hair abrades my nipples, where they rub Tyler's chest, causing me to wiggle more, pressing my sensitive lower lips against hard belly and the happy trail narrowing toward a happily growing cock.

Around us, the gentle bubble of hot spring adds an illicit thrill to sitting flesh to flesh, naked in nature.

"How do you like the hot springs?" Tyler asks, growling into my neck. He nips at the sensitive tendon, driving me out of my freaking mind.

"Not fair.... You know... that's my... spot."

His chuckle vibrates against my skin, adding to the sensualness of rubbing our nude bodies together under water. I hold his head tight, feeling high as the blood rushes under my skin. He's leaving marks and I love it. The man drives me to insanity, healing the parts of me broken before, building confidence through distraction, because all he needs is one touch to wipe my brain of all other thoughts.

Sliding my hand between us, I grab his rigid length and stroke. Tyler hisses, lifting his head to capture my lips. His hands dive into my wet hair, locking it in one fist to hold out of his way.

"Now, baby."

I hold back for a few strokes, pumping the velvety skin over hard steel, watching his jaw lock as his eyes close. Inside, anticipation tightens my core around nothing, increasing my impatience. I lift, centering myself over that thick cock and wait until Tyler's eyes fly open, burning with passion and promises. Like that, locked in each other's grasp, I slide down, engulfing his thickness in one smooth motion.

"Shit..." Tyler's fingertips dig into my hips, holding me still at the base of his cock.

Tilting back and forth, I groan at the pressure against my walls. "So... full..." My engorged clit tingles against Tyler's closely cropped hair and I still, my insides clenching at the intrusion.

Finally, I can't take the pressure and raise myself, lifting nearly off before Tyler takes control, guiding my hips in a steady rhythm. Our breaths mingle, our mouths locked in an open kiss as our bodies rock.

"Mel..." Strain tightens the corner of those melted chocolate eyes. He swells, stealing my breath.

"Yes! Let go, Tyler." My hips pump faster, chasing that release. His jaw clenches as he takes over, slamming our bodies with a force I can't match.

Water squishes obscenely between us.

A few thrusts and I explode like a volcano, clenching his length as I ride the wave.

"Fuck, Mel!" Tyler locks us together, his cock swelling as he comes, rope after rope heating my insides, even in the warm spring.

Our bodies writhe together, breath panting as we come down off that high. I push back, looking up to the sky for some much-needed oxygen. Tyler reaches up, cupping my cheek and I smile, euphoria floating through my body as real as my breasts floating in the water.

Laughter bubbles up. I can't help it. "Outdoor sex."

Tyler's eyes crinkle as he smiles. "That one's a first for me, too."

I clap. "Yay... I never get to knock out your 'never-evers'."

He smirks. "Hey, I may have done crazier shit than you, but the last time I skinny dipped, Smith and I were dumb nine-teen-year-olds on leave." His large hands span across the lower curve of my butt, making me squirm as he leans forward and nips my chin. "You're a lot prettier."

I chuckle. "I hope so."

Carefully, Tyler lifts me off his deflating cock and turns me sideways on his lap, tucking my sweaty hair behind my ear. "There's another first you've given me," he says, his face growing serious.

I wait, snuggling into the crook of Tyler's arms. "What's that?"

His thumb moves up, stroking my cheek. "I love you, Melanie. I have for a while, and I wanted to give you time." His voice rushes, "I'll still give you time... but you need to know, because I'm not going anywhere."

My heart rate kicks to high gear, making words impossible, and I lean forward, capturing Tyler's lips. He sighs, shoulders slumping as if expecting bad news. Silly man. Pulling back, I scan those beautiful eyes. All the ways Tyler has shown his love over these past months hit me at once and my eyes water. "Tyler..." I swallow. "I love you, too."

A smile brightens his face as he pulls mine in, capturing my lips in a searing kiss. We hold there, snuggling closer, reveling in the comfort of admitting our feelings.

When we pull back, neither of us can hide our happiness and Tyler tucks me against his chest, resting his chin on my head.

"So, what *did* you have planned for this weekend?"

"Umm, fix my website, clean, shower, shop. Work, work, clean."

He chuckles. "Wow. You really know how to party," he dead-pans, and I laugh, stroking a palm across the stubble already growing thick this afternoon.

"Guess that means I gotta keep you around, huh?"

Tyler's bright smile amps my excitement as he attempts to smack my ass under the water, and I giggle. "You're stuck with me, woman." He squeezes around my waist and I sigh.

"There's no place I'd rather be, Tyler."

I hope you enjoyed Tyler & Melanie's happily ever after.

Remember, **REVIEWS** are the best gift you can give an author. :)

SUNSHINE & SABOTAGE

NEXT in line for Sunshine Season... Sunshine & Soulmates

Also, don't forget to preorder Tucker's story in Bourbon &

Boss

Epilogue

Tyler

I have never been more thankful for my uncle than I am today. Riding high on the back of finishing another project, I scan the space I created out of sweat and imagination. Tucker gave me carte blanche to execute the vibe he wanted for his rooftop extension to *Two-Fourteen.*

I think it turned out perfect, if I do say so myself.

Fat Edison bulbs hang zigzag across the roof, connecting large cedar pillars. Wispy, sage curtains billow in the crisp fall breeze around wooden dining tables. Couches and bulbous chairs circle the gas firepit for happy hours and hang outs. It's a perfect hideaway for a romantic evening with the greenery Dad picked out, blocking the view of downtown Kissing Springs.

In the summer, we'll install misters around the edge to keep everyone cool, but this time of year, protection from the bitter cold is more important. Umbrella heaters scattered across the space make the temperature tolerable, but I worry about dinner later. Hopefully, the blankets I stored in baskets along the side help. Liza gave me the recommendation for these fat-looped crocheted things that don't look the least bit warm, but they're fluffy and soft, so what do I know?

Sucking in a deep breath, I imagine the smile on Melanie's face when I show her this oasis. Music and great food will fill the space, setting our romantic scene for the most important question of my life. My palms sweat just thinking about it.

Everything needs to be perfect.

Shit! Should I have planned something more elaborate? A hot-air balloon. Something public and crazy.

"Stop second-guessing," I say to the empty roof.

Melanie would hate a public display. If there's one thing I know about my girl, having all eyes on her during an emotional moment would be torture.

Tonight's private dinner will be perfect.

With a lighter heart, I give Tucker's rooftop one last scan, itching to move the hours. There's not much to do between now and then... wash my truck, shower, and shave. Boom. Done. I don't know how I'll survive so many hours until dinner with this ring burning a hole in my pocket.

Pulling away from Melanie's apartment with her scent filling my cab soothes the frazzled edges of my nerves. Her smile lights up the evening sky, shining brighter than the streetlights beaming off the pumpkins and hay bales decorating downtown.

"How did the job go this morning?" she asks. Her curiosity triggers a flash of guilt over lying about my location today.

Surprises don't count as lies, right?

"It was great. I think everyone will be happy with the turnout." There, that's not a lie.

Melanie squints her eyes at me like I've grown two heads, and I laugh, remembering my alibi for the morning was fixing Ms. Betty's busted sewer. I needed a repair that would keep me busy and out of pocket all day. Now, I can't help but laugh as we parallel park beside Two-Fourteen, and I think about what I just said.

Before Melanie can question my sanity, I hop out of my truck and jog to her door. My heart pounds in my chest as I help her down, stopping to admire the cat-like glow to her eyes. "You look beautiful," I say, lifting her chin for a soft kiss. It would be a shame to mess up her lipstick, but I can't resist a taste.

Her maroon wrap dress hugs every curve I want to make mine later tonight. The neckline plunges, revealing the glorious cleavage I love to bury my face in. Those freckles sprinkled across her collar bone call for my tongue to connect the dots. But that will wait for later. I pinch my thigh to keep myself in check, because the love shining up at me under that smokey shadow is a shot straight to the heart.

In a few short hours, if all goes my way, and I'm not insanely delusional, this woman will be mine.

Upstairs, Melanie's gasp swells a sweet pride in my chest. Her mouth hangs open as she takes in the scene I laid out. "It's un-real..." Slowly, Melanie strokes a hand across the back of a wood chair, her skirt twirling as she turns a full circle, a glowing beacon in the moonlight.

"I wanted everything to be perfect," I say, pulling out her chair. "We are officially the first patrons of *Two-Fourteen's* new rooftop terrace."

"Holy cow!" she giggles. "What favor did you promise to pull first dibs?"

A grin spreads so big my cheeks hurt. "I built the place."

"Wow..." Melanie's laughter fades as the server assigned to our table, the one I trusted with a very expensive ring on the way in, fills our water glasses and arranges napkins on our laps.

"Thank you." The waitress gives me a knowing smile.

She pops the cork on the bottle of wine I preordered for dinner and pours a taste in my glass. I take a quick sip, not. "I'll be right back with your starters."

Melanie gives me a funny look, and I can't help but grin. "I gave Tucker a green light on our menu. I hope you don't mind."

"Not at all! Everything that comes out of that kitchen is gold." I join in Melanie's laughter as she sips her wine, relaxing as excitement lights her face.

"My uncle would love to hear that, and I'd say don't make his head bigger, but the man deserves every ounce of praise after all he's done for me."

She reaches for my hand. "He loves the crap out of you, Ty. Every time he talks about you, it's all bragging about your work around town and at the center."

I glance at our entwined fingers, stroking the soft skin between her knuckles. My face is warm, despite the bite in the air. "Are you warm enough?" I ask, hoping to change the subject off myself. The space heaters and fire towers are lit, but I need to do something with my sweaty hands other than fidget on the table.

Where is our waitress? I'm dying to get to dessert. There's no way I'll make it without blurting out everything I want to say too soon?

"I'm fine, Tyler. Where did you go?"

I smile at the sweet worry in those gorgeous eyes. "I'm right here with you. Don't worry about that." Melanie's shoulders sag a bit and I realize I'm ruining the night already just by fussing over every little detail.

Before I can explain, our server appears with a tray of bacon-wrapped scallops and Melanie gasps. "Oh my god! Those look amazing!"

"Enjoy." The girl's ponytail bounces as she practically jogs back to the stairwell. She's not my focus, though.

Melanie lifts her fork and gives me a challenging smirk. "If you want in on this, you better act fast, big boy."

Grinning, I bend forward, threading my fingers through those dark curls cascading down her back. "I may have requested them special for you, so have at it, babe." Sunshine beams from my girl, swelling my pride, and I pull her close, tasting the sweet wine lingering on her pouty lips.

The kiss deepens, and I swallow a delicious moan that sends all my blood south. Our tongues dance sensuously, twirling and reveling in big emotions that have grown in the past months. Each swipe honors the foundation we've built. A foundation for our future that begins tonight.

Minutes pass in a fog until I realize our food's getting cold, and I pull back, soaking in the love shining back at me. "Tucker would kick my ass if I let his food get cold."

Melanie giggles as she spears the tiny disk on her fork. "Fine. Fine. I'll share, but you better reward me later."

I'm smiling as I take my own bite and watch Melanie dig into her plate with gusto. *If she only knew.*

After what feels like hours and twenty courses later, I want to strangle my uncle.

Okay, it's not twenty, and every damn dish tasted of pure sin. But every time Melanie moaned, my cock twitched, wanting to get in on the action. And every specially timed delivery by our waitress delayed the main event.

I try my best to give Melanie a night to remember. I wrapped a quilt over her lap when she shivered, refilled wine, shared my charred mushrooms and made a mental note to add them to her favorites. Soft jazz floats behind our conversation, easing the tension building in my neck as I watch Melanie sway.

Finally, Leah carefully approaches our table with the most beautiful dessert I've ever seen. I grin, waiting impatiently for the girl to sit the massive chocolate globe in front of us on the table. I scan the intricate presentation, wondering exactly where the hell the ring is hidden.

Leah smiles, placing a miniature stainless-steel pitcher closer to Melanie's side. "When you're ready, just drizzle this sauce over the top of the ball and enjoy."

"Oh, wow! Thank you so much," Melanie says, her mouth slightly ajar as she eyes the massive ball that's larger than our plate.

"Would you like more wine?"

"No. I'm fine. Thank you."

The young girl fills my glass and actually winks before she saunters off and leaves me to my moment. *Shit!* My heart rate kicks up as Melanie poses the liquid over our dessert.

"Do you want the honors?"

"All you, baby." I smile, unable to take my eyes off her as she starts to pour. Blood rushes through my ears, roaring louder than Niagara Falls. The lump in my throat threatens to choke me as the first piece of chocolate falls to the bowl underneath.

Melanie swirls the sugary liquid with a flourish, looking like a kid on Christmas morning. Every drizzle causes more and more pieces to break away until all that's left is pieces of chocolate swimming in a bath of caramel liquor with cookie crumbles and decorative berries littering the bottom.

"Oh my god!" The shocked gasp slips out as Melanie's trembling hand flies to her mouth. Her eyes widen into massive green saucers before they fill with tears. Questions flood their depths as she stares at the velvet box revealed by our dessert play. "What is this?"

Smirking, I take the box from its platform and hold it between us, but my smile falls as a tear slips over the heart-shaped curve of Melanie's cheek. "Mel, I love you. I never in my wildest dream imagined I would find a woman who completes me the way you do. Who challenges me and supports me. Who lifts me up and soothes my rough edges. When I met you, I knew you were it for me." I swallow thickly.

"You inspire me to be a better man because you deserve the best. That amazing heart of yours needs to be protected, and I knew from day one that I'd never let another man near it. There's no one alive who will love you more, Melanie. If you let me, I'll spend the rest of my life proving that to you."

Tears free flow down Melanie's face, now, and I wipe them away with my thumb, kissing away a few stragglers as my own eyes blur. Sucking in a deep breath, I bring her forehead to mine, needing to finish this before I'm a blubbering baby.

"Melanie, I promise you, I'm yours. Until my last breath. Will you be mine? Be my wife." I pop open the box in my hand, offering the ring I designed special for her. Melanie's eyes never leave mine, though, and even through the tears, all I see is happiness.

I wait, not daring to breathe until her head shakes in my hand and Melanie launches herself into my lap. "Yes! Yes! I love you so much!"

"Thank God!" My cheeks ache as I slide the shiny silver band on her finger. Perfect fit.

"It's beautiful."

"You're beautiful…"

The night's stress whooshes out of me as her arms circle my neck, and our mouths collide in a frenzy of whispered affirmations and love. Heat simmers under the surface. But this moment is about more than wanting to toss Melanie across my bed. This is about forever.

DON'T FORGET, if you enjoyed Melanie & Tyler's story, please consider leaving a review **HERE**...

If you want to find out more about our hunky chef, Tucker... download **BOURBON & BOSS.**

His kitchen is in disarray, but instead of fixing the problem, Tucker can't take his mind off his tasty pastry chef. She went from

off limits to

impossible to resist.

Once he gets his hands on her, one taste won't be enough.

Also By Annie

BIG PAW MOUNTAIN SERIES

Shattered Illusions: A Bear Shifter Paranormal

Romance

Beyond Expectations: A Bear Shifter +

Firefighter Paranormal Romance ← Sign up for preview & get

notified on release day!

DIXON DRAGON MAFIA

Unleashed: Dixon's Dragon Mafia

WELCOME TO KISSING SPRINGS

- Salty Santa - https://amzn.to/3xMEOU9

-Sunshine & Sabotage – https://amzn.to/3X03iox

-Bourbon & Boss – https://amzn.to/3nXSZnW

Follow The Kissing Springs Book Babes

Join us in our Facebook group, celebrating all things about the

small town of Kissing

Springs, and our steamy book series.

We share recipes, cocktails, tips, freebies, cover reveals, author insights, and more fun.

Go to: Welcome to Kissing Springs Reader Group on Facebook.

The Welcome to Kissing Springs Series

Santa Season   **Sunshine Season**

Bourbon Season   **Midnight Season**

About the Author

Annie Rae

Annie is a wife and mom, living in Texas with her two amazing kiddos, dogs, bunnies, and the sexiest, suited, mountain-man a girl could dream to be her prince (beard included).

Weekends are for cheering on the kiddos in all their craziness and curling up with a steamy romance book and missing too much sleep because of it. The self-proclaimed sunflower would love nothing more than to be on a beach, writing her day away.

Annie loves escaping into great novels where you ride the ride and feel the emotions of great characters, laughing with them, crying with them, and missing them after "the end." It is a dream come true to be able to write about those protective heroes, fated love, and happy endings.

Follow Annie for more fabulous book boyfriends and playful laughs.

www.AuthorAnnieRae.com